TRANSFORMING SNOWRIDGE

Stonefire Dragons Universe
Book 2

JESSIE DONOVAN

Mythical Lake Press, LLC

Transforming Snowridge
Copyright © 2019 Laura Hoak-Kagey
Mythical Lake Press, LLC
Print Edition

Cover Art by Laura Hoak-Kagey of Mythical Lake Design
ISBN: 979-8891560277

The Stonefire and Lochguard series intertwine with one another. (As well as with one Tahoe Dragon Mates book.) Since so many readers ask for the overall reading order, I've included it with this book. (This list is as of January 2024.)

Persuading the Dragon (Stonefire Dragons #12)
Treasured by the Dragon (Stonefire Dragons #13)
The Dragon Collective (Lochguard Highland Dragons #8)
The Dragon's Bidder (Tahoe Dragon Mates #3)
The Dragon's Chance (Lochguard Highland Dragons #9)
Summer at Lochguard (Dragon Clan Gatherings #1)
Trusting the Dragon (Stonefire Dragons #14)
The Dragon's Memory (Lochguard Highland Dragons #10)
Finding Dragon's Court (Stonefire Dragon's Universe #3)
Taught by the Dragon (Stonefire Dragons #15)
Winter at Stonefire (Dragon Clan Gatherings #2)
Masked Dragon of Snowridge (Stonefire Dragons Universe #4) / Jan 2024
Charming the Dragon (Stonefire Dragons #16) / 2024

Short stories that lead up to *Persuading the Dragon* / *Treasured by the Dragon*:

Meeting the Humans (Stonefire Dragons Shorts #1)
The Dragon Camp (Stonefire Dragons Shorts #2)
The Dragon Play (Stonefire Dragons Shorts #3)
Dragon's First Christmas (Stonefire Dragons Shorts #4)

Semi-related dragon stories set in the USA, beginning sometime around *The Dragon's Discovery* / *Transforming Snowridge*:

The Dragon's Choice (Tahoe Dragon Mates #1)
The Dragon's Need (Tahoe Dragon Mates #2)

Stonefire Dragons

Charming the Dragon / Hayley & Nathan (SD #16 / 2024)

Stonefire Dragons Shorts

Meeting the Humans (SDS #1)

The Dragon Camp (SDS #2)

The Dragon Play (SDS #3)

Dragon's First Christmas (SDS #4)

Stonefire Dragons Universe

Winning Skyhunter (SDU #1)

Transforming Snowridge (SDU #2)

Finding Dragon's Court (SDU #3)

Masked Dragon of Snowridge (SDU #4 / Jan 25, 2024)

Tahoe Dragon Mates

The Dragon's Choice (TDM #1)

The Dragon's Need (TDM #2)

The Dragon's Bidder (TDM #3)

The Dragon's Charge (TDM #4)

The Dragon's Weakness (TDM #5)

The Dragon's Find (TDM #6)

The Dragon's Surprise / Dr. Kyle Baker & Alexis (TDM #7 / TBD)

Asylums for Magical Threats

Blaze of Secrets (AMT #1)

Frozen Desires (AMT #2)

Shadow of Temptation (AMT #3)

Flare of Promise (AMT #4)

Cascade Shifters

Convincing the Cougar (CS #0.5)

Reclaiming the Wolf (CS #1)

Cougar's First Christmas (CS #2)

Resisting the Cougar (CS #3)

Love in Scotland

Crazy Scottish Love (LiS #1)

Chaotic Scottish Wedding (LiS #2)

WRITING AS LIZZIE ENGLAND

(Super sexy contemporary novellas)

Her Fantasy

Holt: The CEO

Callan: The Highlander

Adam: The Duke

Gabe: The Rock Star

Chapter One

Rhydian Griffiths couldn't help but smile at the small boy sitting at his kitchen table as he pretended to feed a stuffed toy rabbit some oatmeal.

For the past three months, Rhydian had been taking care of the orphaned boy named Rian Maguire. While the Department of Dragon Affairs had put out notices for the boy's relatives to claim him, no one had yet shown up to do so.

It was entirely possible Rian didn't have any family left alive. Or, at least ones who wanted to acknowledge the relationship since he was half human and half dragon-shifter.

After all, most humans would be afraid, wary, or even disgusted of raising such a child.

Rhydian's dragon spoke up. *If no one has put in a claim by now, they probably won't. We should officially adopt him.*

If anyone had told Rhydian three months prior that

he might be adopting a child, he would've laughed at the absurdity.

However, between the boy's enthusiasm for dragons and the oft-hidden sadness, Rian Maguire had wormed his way into Rhydian's heart.

He wanted to keep the boy and teach him how to be an honorable dragonman.

His dragon grunted. *Good. Then it's decided. You should tell him.*

Before Rhydian could reply to his beast, Rian laid down his spoon and wiped his stuffed rabbit's mouth with a napkin. "Good job, Mr. Cottontail. Rhydian says eating our porridge will make us grow big and strong. And will also make us pay attention better." The little boy lowered his voice. "And if we're lucky, it might even make my dragon talk with me soon, too."

It took everything Rhydian had to keep a smile on his face. The boy had been kidnapped by a splinter dragon hunter group almost four months ago—one of the worst enemies to all dragon-shifters in the UK and Ireland—and no one knew if the bastards had experimented on Rian or not. Some of the other children kidnapped at the same time had received injections that had messed with their dragon-halves, to the point they had gone silent for a time. However, Rian hadn't shared much from his time in captivity beyond the fact he'd seen his parents murdered. And since Rhydian was the adult the boy trusted most, if Rian hadn't told him, he probably hadn't told anyone.

The resulting trauma was hard enough on someone so young, but if Rian had indeed been used as a guinea pig, then it was possible the boy had lost his dragon forever.

Meaning the inner beast would never speak to him, or allow Rian to shift.

No. Rhydian didn't want that for his charge. His head doctor was working with the other British dragon doctors, trying to find cures to the various drugs their enemies had concocted over the years.

In other words, Rhydian had hope.

His dragon sighed. *Why did it take a small lad to make you hope for anything again?*

What are you talking about? I've had hope for years. Otherwise, I never would've tried for the leadership position.

Hope for the clan is different than hope for ourselves. You want Rian to be whole. Not only for his sake, but also for us, so that we can teach him how to be a good dragon-shifter male.

One of the downsides to having a second personality constantly inside your head was that a dragon-shifter could almost never keep secrets truly to themselves. Well, unless they spent a vast amount of effort to do so. Rhydian replied, *Since we'll never have a mate, he'll be our only charge and family. So of course I want the best for him.*

His beast paused a second—never a good sign—before replying, *Then stop stalling, and claim him as our son. File the paperwork today. It'll convince the boy that he has a place to call home again.*

Rian stood and walked over to Rhydian, preventing him from replying to his beast. Rian lifted his stuffed rabbit and said, "Tell Mr. Cottontail he'll grow big and strong, Rhydian. He ate all his oatmeal, just like you said he should."

The toy was a sort of therapy for the boy, and Rhydian had long ago decided to play along until Rian healed a bit more. He fixed his gaze on the gray rabbit with slightly matted fur. "I'm proud of you, Mr. Cottontail. However, if you want to see my dragon later today, then you need to put your bowl in the sink, too."

Rian squealed and ran back to his dirty bowl. Before Rhydian could do more than blink, the boy had put the bowl in the sink and raced back. "When can we see your dragon? In two minutes? Five? Right now?"

Rhydian smiled. "After school. You know how your teachers don't like you missing class, especially since you're a little behind the other students."

Rian sighed loudly. "But maths is no fun. Or writing. Or human studies."

Rhydian had been careful about not dangling something he couldn't promise in the months since Rian had arrived on Snowridge. However, since the three months for the boy to be claimed had expired yesterday, he could finally admit his decision. "If you're to live on Snowridge, you need to learn all of that. Being part of a clan means you need to be the best you can be. But you can't do that until you figure out what you're good at. School helps you discover what your special skills are."

Rian's eyes widened and he jumped in place. "I get to stay on Snowridge?"

He ruffled the boy's hair. "From today, you'll be staying here. With me, if you want to."

"I do!" Rian wrapped his arms around Rhydian's waist. "You, me, and Mr. Cottontail will make our own family. And that way, I won't be alone again."

Rhydian's heart twisted every time the boy brought up his parents. He still didn't know how much he'd seen when it came to his parents' death—Rian's father had been a dragon-shifter, who had been drained of blood—but one day he'd find out.

"You're not alone, lad. I'm here."

Rian hugged him tighter and Rhydian placed a hand on the boy's head.

He had never expected to be a father. However, taking care of Rian over the last three months had been some of the best moments of his life. Well, best ever since he'd lost his love all those years ago.

And even though he hadn't been strong enough to claim the human female he'd loved back then, he'd do everything within his power to protect the half-human boy. Rian Maguire was his family now. And as any dragon-shifter knew, a parent protecting their child was a fierce thing indeed.

DELANEY MURPHY WATCHED as the black taxi cab drove back down the windy mountain road. Only when it was out of sight did she finally turn toward the steep path that should take her to Clan Snowridge's land.

Getting to the remote dragon-shifter clan in

northern Wales had taken her three days longer than expected.

Which meant she was a day past the deadline to collect her nephew.

Some of her friends had tried to dissuade her because he was part dragon-shifter. Needless to say, most of those people weren't her friends anymore.

Rian was her late sister's only child—and only living family member—which made him the only link Delaney still had to her older sister Rosaleen.

As she started up the trail, she tried her best not to think of her late sister. The one she hadn't seen for nearly a decade, ever since Rosaleen had run off with a dragonman she'd wanted to spend her life with.

Over the years, Delaney had occasionally received a letter from her sister, giving her a mini-update about her life in mostly vague terms. However, no matter how often she'd tried to convince Rosaleen to meet in person, her sister had always declined. And since Rosaleen's letters had come from different areas in eastern Ireland, it wasn't as if Delaney could go to the postmarked location, show pictures of her sister, and ask if anyone had seen her.

Even if she'd known Rosaleen's location, it still would've been difficult to connect. Her sister had illegally run away and eloped with a dragon-shifter. While there was talk about the rules changing in Ireland, so that humans and dragon-shifters could marry freely as long as they reported the union to the Irish Department of Dragon Affairs, it hadn't happened yet. As such, it'd taken Delaney longer than expected to prove Rosaleen was her sister, and therefore Rian Maguire was her nephew, especially since it had required both the Irish and British DDA offices to work together.

She kicked a small rock over the edge of the path and then another. Just remembering about how much time she'd wasted on DNA tests and interviews made her angry. And the last thing she wanted was for her temper to show when she finally met the Welsh dragon clan leader.

So she continued to kick rocks, each one helping to release her tension a little bit more. While a punching bag would've been better, she made do with what she had available.

By the time she reached the imposing metal gate emblazoned with the word Snowridge, Delaney had to take a second to catch her breath. Remote wasn't enough to describe how tucked away this dragon clan was. Why couldn't her nephew be with the clan in the Lake District? Stonefire was easy to find, especially these days—what with all the news reports and interviews that kept popping up on the telly.

Taking one last breath, she straightened and readjusted the bag on her shoulder. She had a feeling the dragons already knew she was there, but she still banged on the door. After about fifteen seconds, a Welsh male voice blared from some sort of hidden intercom. "Who are you and what do you want?"

The voice had been irritated and a little restrained. Just her luck, all the dragons in Wales would be grumpy and/or hate all humans. "My name is Delaney

Murphy. I'm here to collect my nephew, Rian Maguire."

After a long pause, the male voice continued, "If that were true, the DDA would've told us you'd be coming."

Her temper inched up a bit, but she somehow kept her tone even, masking her irritation. "I filed all the paperwork and even have my documents here with me. Can't you at least let me in to wait whilst you check them and contact the DDA if need be? It's not like I can easily go to a hotel and wait for you to do it."

"Hold on."

She bit the inside of her cheek to keep her reply from coming.

Just fucking great. Her poor, orphaned nephew was staying with strangers—dragon strangers, nonetheless—and the only thing standing in the way of her collecting him and letting him know everything would be better from now on was some bloody bureaucratic mistake.

As she waited, Delaney paced back and forth in front of the gate. She should conserve her energy given the altitude and how cold it was in the mountains of Snowdonia. But moving helped her to focus and keep from saying something she shouldn't.

Maybe in the future, she should bring a jump rope or something with her, just in case she needed the distraction. It'd always helped her focus during her younger days, when she'd been a boxer.

The same voice finally spoke up a few minutes later. "You can come inside provided you stick with your escorts. They'll take you to a secure location to wait until we have a verdict."

The gates creaked open to reveal a female with brown hair and a male with dark hair standing right next to her, his arms crossed over his chest. Even though they wore coats which covered their arms and any sort of tattoos—adult dragon-shifters always had tattoos on one of their upper arms—their height all but told her they were dragons. And probably security forces, too, judging by their don't-take-any-shite looks.

The female spoke first. "Come with us quietly and save your questions for later. We need to verify your story before anything else."

Delaney had no choice but to follow the order. As she walked between the two tall individuals, she barely had time to notice the large open area beyond the gate before they entered a door on the side of the mountain.

She'd read about how the Welsh dragons lived in a series of cave-like rooms, but as they went inside the door, her mouth fell open.

Instead of stone, the walls were covered in decorative tapestries. Each side told a different story. One seemed to be about a dragon owning and then losing a golden necklace. The other side was vaguer, something to do with dragons in Wales, if the mountains were anything to judge by.

She'd nearly forgotten about how she had two escorts until they stopped in front of an old, solid wooden door. The female dragon-shifter spoke again. "You'll wait in here."

They opened the door and shoved her inside before

she could make so much as a peep. As the door slammed shut, the sound echoed inside the small room.

While it had lights and a small window, everything about the room was functional—a simple table, a chair, and a pile of blankets on the floor with a pillow. There was also a small toilet and sink along the back wall.

In other words, her waiting room was a prison cell.

The DDA had warned her that the Welsh dragons were distrustful of humans, but throwing her in jail was bloody ridiculous. How could one woman be a threat to someone—or, rather, an entire clan of someones— who could shift into a fucking dragon?

However, fuming and cursing to an empty room wouldn't help her. No, she'd save her energy and then let the clan leader have it once they confirmed her story with the DDA. The English and Scottish dragon clans were always banging on about how humans and dragons needed to be more understanding of one another. Snowridge must not have received that message, and maybe they needed the reminder. Especially since they had only recently become allies with the other British dragon clans and probably didn't want to ruin that relationship if they could help it.

Delaney sat on the pile of blankets, settled against the wall, and took out her final letter from her sister. She knew the words by heart, but hearing Rosaleen's voice inside her head one last time would give her the courage to be brave and face the dragon clan leader.

True, she'd never lacked courage before. But facing a human opponent in a boxing ring was a hell of a lot different than facing a man who could turn into a mythical creature and tear her apart with his teeth.

Opening the folded paper, she read her sister's desperate words one last time to give her that extra bit of courage she needed.

Chapter Two

Rhydian stared at the computer screen in front of him and debated what to do.

A human female had shown up on Snowridge, stating she was Rian's aunt. A little digging by one of his Protectors had shown that she'd done as she'd said and submitted paperwork to the DDA to claim Rian as her kin.

Rationally, he knew she was Rian's family and he should hand over the little boy.

And yet, the thought of sending Rian away after telling him he could stay made him hesitate.

His dragon spoke up. *The easiest thing would be to dismiss her and send her back down the mountain. She did miss the deadline after all.*

By one day. And given how difficult it is to find Snowridge, I can understand how.

Don't tell me you're going to give Rian to her. He's our son in all but name. He should stay.

He ran a hand through his hair. *I* want *him to stay. But I should give the female a chance.*

I say fight for custody. Especially since she's human, and she probably doesn't understand how claiming Rian means that she has to live permanently with a dragon-shifter clan.

That detail had been buried in the fine print of the contract the human—Delaney Murphy—had signed. Maybe she'd seen the clause, but he highly doubted it given how minuscule the text had been. *And if she doesn't care about that? Then what?*

His dragon huffed before muttering, *Then I suppose she could stay here.*

Well, Snowridge is more stable than the clan near Dublin in Ireland where she's from, or most of the Irish clans right now, to be honest.

Many of the clans in Ireland were in the process of picking new clan leaders. On top of that, they were under constant surveillance and monitoring by the Irish DDA. Not that Rhydian could blame the human oversight department. After all, two of the Irish dragon-shifter leaders had been hell-bent on killing the female leader, Teagan O'Shea, and had ended up dead themselves. The DDA needed to ensure peaceful transitions and good behavior for PR purposes, to avoid any sort of revolt or outcry by the human population.

His dragon grunted. *We don't know if the human is even brave enough to endure staying on Snowridge for any length of time, let alone anywhere else. Maybe invite her to stay for a trial period, and after she sees how distrustful of humans most of the clan are, she'll leave.*

But she could leave with Rian if the DDA overrides our adoption claim and helps her find somewhere else to stay. And as much as I'm learning to trust Stonefire, I bet they'd take her and the boy if asked.

Technically, no, she couldn't take him. She missed the deadline. And we submitted adoption paperwork an hour before the human showed up. Given how Rian is half dragon-shifter, the DDA will probably rule in our favor.

He sat back in his chair. His dragon's suggestion to kick the female out and keep Rian would be the easiest, but the human female's appearance brought up another issue he'd wanted to tackle—to change how his clan viewed and acted toward humans.

Snowridge's population had suffered as a result of shunning human mates over the last few decades. Dragon-shifter offspring skewed male, and not all females wanted to be mothers. Humans had filled the gap in the past, and Rhydian knew they needed to do it again if his clan was to survive long-term.

Delaney Murphy might be the perfect way to introduce humans to his clan and see how the members of Snowridge reacted. Yes, a slow, controlled experiment. After all, it would be easy enough to protect one human. The alternative would be to apply to the DDA for potential human mates, which meant following the new DDA policy of sending a group of females all at once rather than one at a time like in years past.

And ensuring a group's safety would be a hell of a lot more work.

Rhydian stood. *I'll talk with the human female and judge*

her character. If she's strong enough, she may be exactly what I need right now.

But you're not giving up Rian, right?

No. He'll stay here, and it'll be up to Miss Murphy whether she stays with him, too.

Maybe some would think Rhydian was being selfish, or even callous, to want to keep Rian on Snowridge. However, more than him wanting to raise Rian as his son and give him stability, there was a chance Rian didn't have an inner dragon any longer and his beast could emerge later than most other dragon-shifters. And an untrained young dragon boy living among humans would equal chaos.

And possibly death.

No, Rhydian wasn't going to risk it. The best thing for the boy was to remain on Snowridge and not have yet another home and family ripped away from him. The matter of sharing guardianship with the human could be decided later, if she passed muster.

For the time being, as he made his way toward the cell where Delaney was being kept, Rhydian removed any expression from his face. He needed to be rational for his initial meeting with the human female, and maybe even a tad bit intimidating.

He'd give the human a chance, but only on his terms.

DELANEY HAD BARELY FALLEN asleep before the door to her cell opened and the lights turned back on.

With a curse, she sat up and blinked. She'd lost track of how long she'd been inside the room and only knew it was dark outside now.

Her eyes finally adjusted and she glanced up at the visitor.

The male was tall, with dark hair and blue eyes. Maybe some would be intimidated by the three scars on his cheek, but Delaney had researched Snowridge's clan leader before coming.

Rhydian Griffiths may be taller, stronger, and older, but there was no way she would show fear. All that mattered was collecting her nephew and fulfilling the unanswered pleading in her sister's letter.

She stood slowly, taking her time to let the dragonman know she wasn't afraid of him—a feat she'd perfected in her former boxing career. When she finally reached her full height, she was still a head shorter than Rhydian.

When he finally spoke, his voice nearly made her shiver. "Delaney Murphy, sorry for the delay."

She could be polite, but from everything she'd read about dragon-shifters, they appreciated strength and honesty over formalities and speaking in circles. So she raised an eyebrow and replied, "I'm not so sure about that." He blinked, and she continued before he could say a word. "If you truly cared about my well-being, then you would've put me somewhere warmer. And maybe with a bed or sofa instead of a pile of blankets on a hard, stone floor."

Rhydian looked around the room a second before returning his gaze to hers. "We haven't used this room in years. As you know by now, we're in a remote part of Wales. I don't usually need to keep prisoners."

Delaney had no idea why she'd be a big enough threat to merit time in Hotel Prison Cell, but she focused on what was more important. "I have no reason to trouble you any longer than necessary. If you give me a proper room to sleep in tonight, I can take Rian and be off in the morning."

"No."

She frowned at the finality in his tone. "What do you mean no? All of the paperwork should be in order. If your people couldn't find it, I can contact the DDA liaison right now and prove it to you."

He shook his head. "That's not it. We confirmed your paperwork. However, judging by your desire to leave first thing, I'm guessing you didn't read the fine print of the contract you signed."

She clenched her fingers into fists. After everything, there might be another damn obstacle to overcome. "What bloody fine print? I read every word in those documents, so just tell me plainly what you mean."

The dragonman smirked and it took everything Delaney had not to cross the floor and clock him. Hitting the dragon clan leader was most definitely not something she should do.

Besides, that sort of behavior belonged in her old life, the one she'd left because of an injury. The new Delaney Murphy didn't fight anyone unless it was in self-defense.

Clearing her throat, she tried to make her voice

more even and polite. "Please tell me about the fine print."

Rhydian shrugged. "The type is small, maybe too small for human eyes unless you zoom in. I think the DDA does it on purpose." She opened her mouth to ask again, but Rhydian put up a hand and continued. "It says that Rian must live with a dragon clan. It gives any guardian of the boy the option to live with him on any clan inside the UK or Ireland as well, but Rian can't live amongst humans. He's half dragon-shifter. It's too dangerous."

Damn. Taking Rian back to her home near Dublin wasn't an option, nor could she ask the dragon clan near the city for help since they weren't fond or even tolerant of humans. If she kept Rian, she'd have to live elsewhere.

And not just anywhere, but on one of the dragon clan's lands. Maybe not for the rest of her life, but at least until Rian reached adulthood.

Maybe some people would see that as a deal breaker and walk away. However, Delaney had little keeping her back in Carrickmines. She could do her graphic design job anywhere, and she couldn't let her sister down.

Still, it might not have to be inside these bloody cold mountains in Wales. Maybe she should remind the Welsh leader of that and see if he started being nicer toward her or not.

So she straightened her shoulders a little more and said, "It doesn't have to be this clan though, right? You said it can be any clan in the UK or Ireland. And if that's the case, I'm not sure I want to risk being thrown into this cell whenever I irritate someone here. And believe me, that will probably happen often."

He tilted his head. "Irritate them? How?"

Great. She'd gone and hinted at some of her flaws, all within minutes of meeting him. Her sister had been the much more tactful one out of them. And in circumstances like these, Delaney wished she could be a little more like Rosaleen.

Rhydian remained quiet, waiting for an answer. Since there was nowhere to run, Delaney decided bluntness was probably best. "I tend to tell the truth. A wee bit too much, according to others. And since most people don't want to hear it, they get upset, or storm off, or report me to HR."

"I prefer the truth," Rhydian stated.

His eyes flashed to slits and back and Delaney leaned forward. Had his dragon just spoken to him? Her earlier research said the pupils flashed when that happened. "What does your dragon say?"

He raised his brows. "You did some reading about us, I see. Most humans jump back or faint when they see our pupils change."

Even more of the truth slipped out. "I used to be a professional boxer. If I can stomach blood and even a few odd teeth on the ground, I can handle some flashing eyes."

Rhydian took a step closer. "A boxer, you say?"

Most men made a quick exit or turned wary whenever she mentioned how she'd been a boxer. But not Rhydian Griffiths. He was different.

But then of course he was, wasn't he? He was a dragonman.

Not that she was going to let his reaction change her mind about taking Rian and leaving. "Yes. So be forewarned—if you or any of your clan try something, I'll defend myself. You lot living inside a mountain definitely works to my advantage. No sane dragon would shift inside of solid rock."

Rhydian stared at her, his eyes flashing, and remained silent.

But she didn't back down. Confidence was one of the few things she had in the moment, so she stood tall and waited to see how the dragon leader would react.

Delaney Murphy wasn't what Rhydian had expected, that was for certain.

Of all the females to be Rian's aunt, the one in question was a bloody former boxer.

His dragon snorted. *I guess she won't be intimidated easily.*

I thought you wanted her spooked, so she'd flee as soon as possible?

Perhaps. But she's strong, fierce, and beautiful. I want her.

Rhydian did his best not to let his unease show on his face. *You're kidding, right?*

No. Woo her a bit, and then maybe she'll let us kiss her.

His dragon's behavior sent off warning bells. *Fate wouldn't be absurd enough to make this human our true mate, would it?*

Why not? Step a little closer. I want to smell her so we can dream about her later.

Most dragon-shifters would be happy to find their potential true mate.

But for Rhydian, it was an inconvenience. There was too much to do with the clan. Not to mention the last time he'd been with a human female, it had ended with her being chased out of Wales and him being given a reminder by his uncles that he needed to stay away from humans. A reminder that had resulted in the three permanent scars on his cheek.

His dragon spoke up. *Deny it all you want, but you think Delaney is beautiful, too, with her long, dark hair and dark eyes. And her strength, both physical and in terms of her personality, is the opposite of Liliwen.*

Liliwen had been a shorter, curvier female who had been too kindhearted to deal with Snowridge's animosity toward humans. He'd known that from their first accidental meeting, but he'd been young at the time and had thought he could change the world.

But the world was a lot tougher to change than most people realized.

Rhydian replied to his beast, *One of the clan members taking a human mate would be easy. Me doing it, though? There will be rebellion. If she even wants a dragon mate.*

Why wouldn't she? We're quite the catch.

He must've been lost in conversation too long with his dragon because Delaney stepped closer and waved her hand in front of his face. "Pardon me interrupting, but maybe you could tell me what's going to happen?

Because if you're going to lock me up in here again, I'm going to fight you, win, and leave."

His dragon snorted. *She's definitely not afraid of us.*

Rhydian ignored his beast. "Cockiness may have worked in your boxing days, but dragon-shifters are physically stronger than humans."

Delaney turned partially away before she snapped back and moved like lightning toward him. She tried to punch him in the side, but Rhydian grabbed her wrist and twisted her arm behind her back.

For a second, all he could do was stare down at her thrust-out chest, watching the rise and fall of breasts, and revel in the heat from her body.

While absurd, he swore she smelled like summer and sunshine.

His dragon hummed. *She's so close. Tilt her head a little and move in. She might let us kiss her.*

I'm not going to accost her.

Almost to spite his dragon, Rhydian released the human female and moved back to lean against the doorframe. "Dragon-shifters are always quicker, not to mention we have better hearing. Maybe one day you'll think of a strategy to win against me, but today isn't that day, Delaney Murphy."

"But you think I could, which just raised my opinion of you."

Her words shouldn't have made his heart speed up, but they did.

Rhydian could be truly fucked if he hung around this female too much.

His dragon merely laughed, which didn't help matters.

He shrugged. "The fact you made it as close as you did proves you have some skill." She narrowed her eyes, but he beat her to it. "However, do you want to waste time debating how great you are, or do you want to discuss Rian?"

Her body relaxed a fraction. "When can I see him?"

"Has he ever met you? Because I've been taking care of him for the last three months and he's never mentioned having an aunt."

Pain flashed across Delaney's gaze but was gone before Rhydian could blink. "My sister didn't want to risk me getting into trouble via association, so she never let me meet Rian. But he's the only family I have left now." She stood tall again. "Which is why I'm going to take care of him, no matter if it means living with a dragon clan or not."

For a split second, Rhydian was sympathetic. The only family he had left was a cousin and second cousin, and now Rian.

His beast chimed in. *She could be our family, too.*

Stop. I'm not talking about this right now.

"Rian's life has been chaotic recently, what with all that happened to his parents and afterward, so I need to prepare him to meet you." He took a step backward and motioned down the corridor. "However, I'll show you to a decent set of quarters to spend the night. You'll be near my security forces, though, so I'd advise against wandering off."

Delaney snorted. "Advise? You can just tell me plainly that I need to stay in my room. I thought dragon-shifters were more forthright than humans? Or at least that's what I've read."

Her response fascinated him. And stirred something he hadn't wanted to do in a long time—prod and tease her. "What you read about and what is reality are two different things. Or should I ask you if leprechauns are real? Or, maybe ask if you've found a pot of gold at the end of the rainbow?"

She grunted, and Rhydian nearly smiled at the sound. "That means you're a miner or sheep farmer on the side, right? Like all the Welsh."

He grinned. "I think that's still better than being a potato-eating, gold-hunting drunk."

She waved a hand in dismissal. "If you say so. At least I'd be rich, have a plate of chips, and be having a good time."

Rhydian laughed. The female was clever. "While I agree I like that scenario, the Welsh have you beat on one thing, Delaney. They have the best flag in the world."

Delaney rolled her eyes. "Yes, there's a bloody dragon on the Welsh flag. But unless you're a red dragon, it's a bit of a blow, aye? Because it means only red dragons are revered."

Rhydian was a black dragon, but he wasn't about to give the female the advantage. "You'll just have to wait and see what color my dragon is." He gestured again with his hand. "Come. I'll show you to your quarters."

As she walked past him, her scent of summer and

sunshine filled his nose. His beast growled. *Why did you suggest we leave the room? We could've kept her here, talked to her, and maybe she'd have let us kiss her.*

No, dragon. Whether you think she's our true mate or not, I don't care. We can't afford to disrupt the clan by taking a human mate. If she wants to find one in another male, then so be it. We'll have Rian to raise, and that's all that matters.

Liar. You know you want her, too.

With more than thirty years of practice, Rhydian knew how to keep some of his thoughts private.

There was no way in hell he'd let his dragon know that he'd like to put Delaney in a hold again when she was naked, and then he'd slowly torture her before he bent her over and took her from behind.

There was something about her gumption and defiance that stirred his desire. Which he could never act on.

So he needed to stay away from Delaney Murphy as much as possible, and never be alone with her again.

Which, of course, was going to be difficult given how she was Rian's aunt. But if the boy was present in the same area, Rhydian was positive he could forget the female and focus on Rian's welfare only.

He said to the female, "If you let me know what you eat, we can pick up some groceries on the way to your quarters."

"So there's a supermarket inside the mountain?"

He said dryly, "Yes, we even have electricity. And those strange contraptions called phones."

She rolled her eyes—she seemed to do that a lot. "I'm not stupid. There are lights above us, so of course you have electricity. Although no mobile service. I couldn't get a signal in that room."

"You'll be briefed later on what services we have." He paused. "Provided you want to stay, of course."

Delaney searched his gaze. "What's that supposed to mean?"

"It means that you're here on a trial basis, Delaney. Whether you stay or not depends on how you act."

She sighed dramatically. "Please don't tell me that means you'll give me a series of tests."

His dragon chimed in. *That's a good idea. A lot of one-on-one tests. Yes, I like that.*

He didn't dignify his beast with a response. "No worse than what dragons are put through by the Department of Dragon Affairs. As much as I'd like to believe sharing DNA with Rian makes you an innocent human who'd never do me or my clan harm, I can't. As you well know from what happened with your sister and her mate, dragon-shifters—and those associated with them—have to be cautious."

With that, Delaney fell silent, and Rhydian was content to not talk further.

Because if she shared more about herself, he might be tempted to ask for more and more again. And that would lead to what would most likely divide his clan—Rhydian once again wanting a human as his own.

Chapter Three

Delaney hadn't been able to sleep more than a few minutes the night before, so she was dressed and pacing as she waited for her escort to arrive.

To be honest, it probably was better that she hadn't slept. It'd been hard enough keeping the dragon leader out of her mind while awake. Who knew what would've happened if she'd been asleep.

And considering his strong, firm hand easily restraining her, combined with his heat at her back, had made her want to relax and lean against him, she didn't want naked dreams of Rhydian Griffiths tempting her with something she couldn't have.

Rian was her priority. She would live up to her sister's request to look after him like her own. And while Delaney didn't know a lot about being a parent, she knew that a child's needs came first.

Even a one-night fling would overly complicate

things, especially if Rian had formed any sort of attachment to Rhydian. And considering how the Welsh leader had been taking care of the lad for three months, it was possible he already saw Rhydian as a father figure.

In other words, Rhydian Griffiths was off-limits.

It wasn't as if he were unique among dragon-shifters. Any of the security forces they called Protectors probably could've done the same thing and deflected her blow, which was something few human men could do unless they were well-trained. And she'd always craved a man who didn't balk at her strength or skill.

Rhydian was strong, yes, but he'd been her first true interaction with a dragon-shifter, nothing more.

A knock on the door made her jump. Taking a deep breath, she walked over and opened it.

A small flicker of disappointment flared when it wasn't Rhydian she found but rather the dark-haired female from the day before. The woman had been one of the two people who'd first escorted her inside the mountain.

The dragonwoman motioned with her head toward the corridor. "Follow me."

By nature, Delaney wasn't a follower. As a boxer, she'd always looked for the best opening, the perfect way to hit and bring down her opponent. She was used to attacking and taking charge.

But for Rian's sake, she'd have to follow orders for who knew how long. The trick would be in not making a misstep that could threaten her chances of staying on Snowridge and looking after Rian. While she could remind Rhydian of her option to live with another dragon clan, she didn't want to move Rian unnecessarily. She needed to give Snowridge a chance for his sake.

So she needed to avoid any trouble, like the kind that could brew from sleeping with the clan leader. Aye, she'd fucked up a bit with Rhydian the night before, possibly encouraging him with her honesty and how her heart had raced when he'd had her in a hold against his body. Delaney just needed to ensure something similar didn't happen again.

Focusing on her surroundings to cleanse her mind of Rhydian Griffiths, Delaney noticed that much like the earlier corridors she'd seen inside Snowridge, the current ones were also lined with tapestries. Maybe she could find out the stories behind them and share them with Rian. After all, kids were supposed to like stories, right?

Not wanting to dwell on how much more she needed to learn as a parent, Delaney pushed all doubts out of her head. Rian seeing her for the first time wouldn't be easy, especially since Delaney looked a lot like her sister. And she needed to prepare for the boy's reaction in case it triggered some sort of painful memory.

Even if it did, she would find a way to help him. She had to, for both her sister and nephew's sake.

The dragonwoman finally stopped in front of a

door set a little apart from all the rest. She knocked, and Rhydian opened the door. He nodded at the dragon-shifter. "Thanks, Carys. I can take it from here."

The woman named Carys didn't budge. "Are you sure, Rhydian? I'd feel better if you'd let me at least stand guard at the door."

"Wren is a few doors down, ready to help if I call. I need you to work on the project I gave you."

Delaney expected Carys to protest as Protectors were supposed to guard their leaders' lives above all else according to something she'd read, but the dragonwoman merely bobbed her head. "Of course."

With that, the female left. Rhydian's blue-eyed gaze finally met hers.

And damn it, his piercing eyes made her insides flip. No man should be as sexy as this one.

His deep voice rolled over her. "Come in. Rian's in his room for now. I'll fetch him once we lay some ground rules."

At the mention of her nephew, the heat and fuzzy feeling vanished. This would be her first chance to make Rian a priority over anything else. "Then let's get started. I don't want to waste any more time before meeting him."

Rhydian stepped aside and she entered the quarters.

Considering they were inside a mountain, it was a lot homier and warm than she'd expected. The walls were covered in wooden panels, which were carved with dragons, flowers, and animals she didn't have time to sort out. All the furniture was in dark colors, and some old swords and shields hung above a fireplace. "This is definitely a single man's home."

"Actually, this is the clan leader's quarters."

She raised an eyebrow. "And have they all been men?"

Rhydian grunted. "Yes, although I don't think that will be the case forever."

His comment piqued her curiosity and she couldn't help but blurt, "Ireland has one female dragon leader. Is Wales gearing up to be the next clan to have one, too?"

"While I think it'll happen one day, I hope not too soon. I have too much to accomplish before giving up my leadership position."

She should absolutely ignore his comment and ask about Rian. But Delaney had no idea if she'd ever get a one-on-one with the clan leader again, without Rian present, so she asked, "Such as what?"

He studied her with guarded eyes, as if he only looked hard enough, he could see inside her brain.

His pupils flashed to slits and back again before he finally replied, "Getting my clan to stop hating humans, for one. You're my best chance of doing that, Delaney. Keep that in mind."

As they stared at one another, she felt glued in place. There was something about this man—as if his quiet power held deeper secrets, ones that drew her to him.

Then Rhydian's eyes darted to her lips and her heart rate kicked up.

By the time his gaze returned to hers, she was tempted to close the short distance between them so she could feel the strong, powerful dragonman's heat again.

Never in her life had she felt such a pull toward another man. Maybe dragon-shifters had some type of magic they could use against humans.

Although a human love potion seemed a bit much.

A little boy raced across the room and stopped right in front of her. Delaney instantly looked down at a little boy that had her sister's eyes.

Which were also her eyes.

Rian had come out before she'd had time to prepare herself, and tears prickled her eyes as she imagined her sister laughing with the little boy in front of her.

Her nephew asked, "Who are you? You're too short to be my mam, and your hair color is different, but you look just like her." Rian looked too Rhydian. "Who is she, Rhydian?"

Rhydian casually placed a hand on the lad's shoulder. The familiar gesture sent a small thread of jealousy through Delaney. She'd been right—Rian had grown attached to the clan leader.

Not waiting for Rhydian to answer, she did. "My name is Delaney Murphy. Your mother was my sister, which makes me your aunt."

Rian's brows furrowed. "Aunt? I thought I didn't

have any family. Mam and Dad always said it was just us three."

Her heart squeezed. Rosaleen hadn't told her that, and even though she was dead and there was nothing she could do about the past, it still hurt.

Rhydian cleared his throat. "Sometimes adults tell small lies, ones that can help protect others."

Rian replied, "But I thought all lies were bad? You always scold me when I lie to you, Rhydian."

"Because your lies aren't protecting anyone but you. And usually it's hiding something bad, like stealing an extra biscuit or not doing your homework."

Rian tilted his head. "So what's the difference?"

"The difference is that your mum and dad didn't want your aunt to get into trouble. I've explained before how a human mating a dragon-shifter in Ireland is against the law. And so to keep your Aunt Delaney safe, they didn't tell you about her."

Rian glanced at her. "Why? I wouldn't hurt her."

Rhydian grunted, garnering the boy's attention once more. "Maybe not on purpose, but sometimes, especially when we're young, we tell secrets we shouldn't."

Rian looked at Delaney again, studying her face.

He looked so much like her sister, Rosaleen, that it hurt—the same nose, the same auburn hair, the same dark brown eyes.

While her sister would live on through Rian, it still pained Delaney to look at the lad. Hearing about her sister's death and meeting face-to-face with her son, knowing neither of them would ever see Rosaleen again, made it all so real.

The tears she'd been holding back were going to fall. Delaney had been hiding her hurt and betrayal at her sister's actions for so long. Why it had to come rushing forth now, she didn't know. However, one thing was for certain—she was on the verge of breaking down and didn't want to do it in front of Rian.

Which meant she needed to escape somewhere private, to save Rian the confusion.

Delaney was just together enough to ask Rhydian, "The toilet?"

He gestured to a door and she rushed for it. As soon as she shut the door, Delaney slid to the ground and did her best to muffle the sobs that came rushing forth.

RHYDIAN STARED at the toilet door, just able to hear Delaney crying.

His dragon spoke up. *We should check on her.*

He wanted to, but he couldn't leave Rian alone. Especially after introducing him to a woman who apparently looked a lot like his mother.

Rian tugged his top. "What's wrong? I hear her crying."

A human wouldn't have been able to hear Delaney's muffled sobs, but then again, Rian was half dragon-shifter. "She just misses her sister, lad. A lot like how you miss your mum."

He shuffled his feet. "Well, when I'm sad, you always take me out and show me your dragon form. Maybe you should try that with her, too. I'm sure Auntie Laney would forget about everything else when you spread your wings."

He smiled at the boy's shortening of Delaney's name. "I don't know if that would work, but if you want to ask her if she wants to see my dragon form, then you can do so."

Rian nodded. "Okay. Wait right here."

As the boy rushed toward the toilet door, Rhydian's beast chimed in. *I didn't think you'd show her our dragon form this soon, if at all.*

She already knows I'm a dragon-shifter, so it's not a big surprise.

You've never been this casual about shifting.

She's in pain. Not even I am going to be a bastard and try to push her away or make her hurt even more when she's crying.

Good, good. That gives me more time to convince you we should kiss her.

Shut it, dragon. She's crying over her dead sister. Now is not the time to think of kissing her.

His beast huffed. *I won't stop thinking about it until you do it. I want her. She'll make the cold, dark winters so much brighter. And warmer. Why wouldn't you want the female by our side?*

Rian rushed over, and Rhydian focused on the boy as he said, "I convinced her. Let's go see your dragon, Rhydian! Oh, wait! I want to get Mr. Cottontail first. He wants to see your dragon, too."

The boy rushed from the room. A second later,

Delaney opened the door. While she wasn't crying, her eyes were still slightly red and puffy.

His dragon growled. *She should never cry.*

While he agreed, he didn't want to encourage his beast. So he walked over to Delaney. "We don't have to do this if you don't want to. It's just that Rian always cheers up when he sees my dragon."

She sniffled and forced a smile. "No, it's okay. I've never seen a dragon up close before, and if I'm going to not only be an aunt to one but also live with a dragon clan, I'd best start getting used to the idea."

Yes, yes, she will. And maybe I can win her over in our dragon form since you're dragging your feet.

Delaney searched his eyes. "Is it rude to ask what your dragon just said?"

He decided to be honest. After all, it was better for her to ask him questions than to offend an older dragonman who thought humans should be pushed off a mountain for being rude. "We usually don't ask unless we know the person well. Our inner dragons are less tactful, and often brutally honest. In most cases, their words are embarrassing.

His beast growled. *It's not embarrassing when it's the truth. I will never understand how the human half works.*

Well if you haven't figured it out in forty years, you probably never will.

With a huff, his dragon turned his back and ignored him.

Rhydian knew he'd have to woo his beast a little to shift, but he reveled in the short span of silence.

Since Delaney was staring at him with her brows raised in question, he said, "Just a little disagreement. That happens a lot between the human and dragon halves."

Rian raced into the room carrying his stuffed rabbit. He jumped in. "Which I think will be great. Like having a friend with you all the time." Before Delaney could ask any questions, Rian held up his toy. "Say hello to Mr. Cottontail. He's my best friend."

"Cottontail?" Delaney touched the button nose. "I had a stuffed rabbit named Mr. Cottontail when I was a child."

"Really? Mam suggested the name. She said it was a special one, and that he would always be my friend, no matter what."

Delaney nodded. "The same for me."

Rhydian sensed there was a story there, but he also could tell Delaney was about to cry again. Since the thought of her sobbing made both man and beast growl, he guided them toward the door. "Come on. All three of you can watch me change into a dragon."

As they walked down the corridor, Rian chatted about Mr. Cottontail eating his breakfast so he could grow big and strong. He even made Delaney laugh.

Rhydian loved the crinkles at the corners of her eyes. She was so bloody beautiful without even trying.

His dragon's actions probably meant she was their true mate. If he ever kissed Delaney, that meant kicking off a mate-claim frenzy that would only end once she was pregnant with his child.

But even if his clan would accept that, there was the matter of Rian. The last thing Rhydian wanted to do was make the boy feel displaced, or even replaced, with a new baby.

His dragon finally turned around again. *We're able to love more than one child.*

Why am I even thinking about this? I can't risk the clan turning chaotic, which would most assuredly happen.

Maybe, maybe not. Just don't push her away and end up regretting it.

As Rian took Delaney's hand—the boy was *still* talking—the sight of the pair walking together did something to his insides.

He said to his beast, *Maybe. I won't turn my back on the idea, but I won't rush into it, either.*

That's better than this morning. I'll just have to work harder at convincing you to give it a chance. The clan is stronger and more unified than you think.

Rhydian wanted to believe it, but too many clans had dissolved into chaos recently—both in Ireland and the one in the South of England, even if the English one was doing better now—that he didn't want Snowridge to be yet another name added to that list.

But the image of Rian and Delaney living with him, the three of them loving each other and doing their best to banish the sadness of the past, was one that tempted him. So much so, Rhydian debated testing the clan's limits.

However, Rhydian would start slowly. Maybe a clan gathering to introduce Delaney would be a good first step. He'd have to talk to his Protectors later and see what they thought.

They rounded the last corner and reached the door leading to the outside landing area. All of his planning and consulting could wait. For a short while, he could simply revel in shifting and sharing his dragon with Delaney for the first time.

Chapter Four

Delaney had nearly forgotten all about her tears by the time she, Rian, and Rhydian reached the outside landing area.

Her nephew was a talker and far more charming than any seven-going-on-eight-year-old should be.

Although she recognized the chatting for what it was—a way to hide his feelings or try to forget about his recent past.

Delaney had done that, too, when she'd been not much older than Rian was now. It'd taken boxing to help her deal with the grief surrounding her younger brother's death and sort through her feelings. While many viewed the sport as merely two people hitting each other, it was so much more. The strategy, the tactics, the decision-making—it all required a lot of concentration and practice. So much so that Delaney hadn't had the time to natter on and on about nothing. To be the best, she had to focus her energy on other things. She eventually realized that when she embraced her feelings, she accomplished so much more in the ring than when she had tried to lock them away.

Doing the same in real life was harder, though, ever since she'd been forced to give up her boxing career. Hence why she'd broken down about her sister earlier.

Rian stopped in place and tugged her hand, the action jarring her from her thoughts. He motioned his stuffed toy rabbit toward the ground. "We need to stay here. Any closer and we could get hurt. Right, Rhydian?"

The Snowridge leader smiled down at the lad, good humor and caring filling his gaze. "Aye, you're right."

He ruffled Rian's head, and Delaney took a second to study the dragonman.

He was far kinder than she'd pictured, especially given Snowridge's reputation as a close-knit clan that didn't take well to strangers.

And yet, he'd taken in a wee Irish boy as his own and hadn't batted an eyelash in acknowledging Delaney's mini-breakdown earlier.

Her eyes fell to his jaw, and then up to the scars on his cheek. She burned to know the details of the story behind them. No doubt they had shaped the man Rhydian had become.

Not that she should care about such things. However, if Rhydian was to be involved in Rian's upbringing, then she most certainly had a right to know a bit about his past.

Rhydian caught her staring, but Delaney didn't look

away. Being coy wasn't her style, and she wasn't about to start now.

The dragonman looked as if he wanted to say something, but he instead looked back at Rian. "Do you remember what I told you about what to do when shifting in front of humans?"

Rian swung his stuffed rabbit to and fro before nodding. "Aye, we ask them to turn around. That way they don't get embarrassed."

She couldn't help but quip, "What? No shifting while still clothed and looking all fierce and mighty?"

Rhydian shrugged. "This is one of my favorite tops. So, no, I'm not going to destroy it to fulfill some fantasy of yours."

She was tempted to say it wasn't a fantasy. But as the image of Rhydian ripping his shirt off to reveal his muscled chest flashed into her mind, she decided maybe it could be. Determined to move the conversation to much safer territory, she said, "So that shirt is a type of treasure, right? That means it's true, then, about dragons hoarding treasures."

Rian asked, "What's hoarding?"

Rhydian never looked away from Delaney's gaze. "It means keeping things forever. Humans like to tell stories about how we only want to collect gold and other treasures and store them in protected places like vaults or mountains. Usually the stories also say that we do all sorts of crazy things to protect the objects, making us look stupid before eventually getting killed."

Rian leaned forward. "Do we do that? Keep stuff? Is there a room full of treasures?"

The corner of Rhydian's mouth ticked up. "Well, there are a few treasures stored in the archives, but those things are fairly worthless to anyone else. And since dragons have to trade and pay for things, just like humans, hoarding gold is fairly impossible."

Grinning, Delaney replied, "And here I thought it'd be fun to try swimming through a room of gold and treasure, just like you see in some of the cartoons. I guess that means striking it from my list of things to do here."

Rhydian raised an eyebrow. "There may or may not be other secrets here. You'll just have to stay around long enough to find out what they are."

Okay, those words piqued her curiosity. Just what kind of secrets did Clan Snowridge possess?

Rian opened his mouth—probably with another question—but Rhydian beat him to it. "If you want to see me shift, it's now or never, lad. I have quite a few things to do today. Do you want me to answer questions, or do you want to see my dragon?"

Even though Delaney knew Rhydian was clan leader with a multitude of duties, she'd nearly forgotten about it. What, with his teasing and easy manner, he wasn't anything like what the rumors on the internet said about him and other dragon-shifter leaders.

Before her thoughts went back down the dangerous path of thinking how much sexier he was than she'd expected, Rian made a circling motion with his finger and said, "Turn around so we can see Rhydian's dragon."

It was on the tip of her tongue to say no. If she was

to live with dragons, she needed to become accustomed to their ways.

Although, secretly she was curious to see what Rhydian looked like without a stitch of clothing. His broad shoulders and lean hips suggested some rather juicy eye candy underneath all those layers.

Not that she should be interested in it. But, hell, it would've been a lie to say she wasn't.

Rian turned so he faced away from Rhydian. "I'll keep you company, Auntie Laney. Come on. The faster you turn, the faster he changes."

Trying her best not to laugh at Rian's attempted serious tone—let alone tear up again at him calling her his aunt—Delaney complied. She strained her ears for any sound as well as scanned the corners of her vision for any sudden bursts of light. There hadn't been much information about how a dragon-shifter changed, let alone any videos. Given how everyone had a camera these days with their phones, it was amazing none existed. The DDA must have a hand in keeping them off the internet to prevent any possible paranoia or fear.

After a few pops, a half roar filled her ears. Turning around, her mouth dropped open.

The black dragon was about four times her height, his scales dark but slightly iridescent at the same time, the faint sunshine making them a multitude of colors.

Even in his dragon form, the scars showed on his cheek. But she barely paid them any heed, especially when Rhydian raised his wings up behind him and spread them.

The sun highlighted the faint veins and bones of the impressive wingspan.

He was powerful, yes, but beautiful, too. She wondered how anyone would want to kill such magnificent creatures simply for their blood and then go sell it on the black market.

Rian cheered. "See? I told you he likes to spread his wings. He won't take me up into the air. But maybe one day, he will. I have to be older, though. Maybe he'll take you up into the sky, too?"

At the thought of flying on a dragon thousands of meters in the air, the blood drained from her face.

The dragon let out a puff of air she swore was a snort.

Clearing her throat, she stood a wee bit taller. "I'm not the best with heights. But given how I don't have wings, I think that's understandable."

The dragon snorted again, somehow making the magnificent creature adorable.

Not that Rhydian would like being called adorable, she bet.

Rian took her hand and tugged. "Come on, Auntie Laney. You need to pet him. He's smooth and a little soft, and not at all cold like the stories say."

She moved with the boy and frowned. "What stories?"

"The ones in the school library. They have heaps and heaps of children's books. But most of them are written by humans, so they're always wrong. I don't always have scales on my back. Or on my feet. Or horns on my head."

Somewhere in the back of her mind, she wondered if the dragon-shifters had thought about writing their own stories and publishing them. It could help dispel the negative stereotypes floating around. And starting with children would be a good first step.

However, they reached Rhydian's dragon form and he gently butted her shoulder, scattering her thoughts about books. Rian translated Rhydian's movement. "He wants you to touch him. Dragons love to be petted and scratched, and so many other things. I'm not sure why they like baths in cold lakes so much, but they do that, too."

She gingerly touched Rhydian's cheek. The slightly warm, smooth surface surprised her, despite Rian's warning.

Gently caressing his cheek, she smiled as the dragon closed his eyes and hummed. He acted like a cat or dog receiving a good scratch.

Rian piped up again. "He's happy. Try scratching behind his ear."

Running her fingers over Rhydian's scales, she finally reached behind his ears. She expected to find more scales, but there was a small patch of skin behind the ear, with no scales over it.

She wondered what other secrets Rhydian's dragon form held.

Careful not to hurt him—hey, it was possible she could hurt the dragon—she ran her nails back and forth against the leathery skin. The dragon's hum increased further, the sound reminding her almost of a loud cat's purr.

Since Rhydian couldn't talk, and even she knew dragons didn't have special telepathic powers, she asked Rian, "So humming is a good thing, right?"

"Yep. But he's humming really loud now. You must be better at scratching and petting than me."

The dragon opened his eyes, the pupils more slitted than before. She murmured, "I wish you could tell me what you're thinking right now."

Rian said, "He can't, silly. But there are dragon signals, loads of them. Once I can shift, I'll have to learn them all." Rian spread his arms and mimicked flying. "I can't wait."

Delaney was still staring into Rhydian's eye and swore she saw sadness there.

Careful to keep her voice low so Rian wouldn't hear her, she stated, "Later, you need to tell me why you're sad all the sudden. I have a feeling it's related to Rian, and I have the right to know."

She expected Rhydian to back away and huff or some such dismissive dragon signal. But he merely nodded.

Then he roared and Rian rushed back. "He wants to change back, Auntie Laney. Come on. We'll stand where it's safe."

She nearly protested that it had only been a few minutes, but Delaney kept her mouth shut. Rhydian no doubt had plenty to do. And if she wanted to talk alone with him later, she shouldn't delay him from his clan leader duties. The sooner he did them, the sooner she could seek him out and corner him to explain a few things.

As she walked back to her original spot and turned her back once more, she wondered what a clan leader did all day.

Despite her research, there was still so much she didn't know about dragon-shifters.

Then an idea sparked. "Rian, once you're done with school, will you help me learn more about Snowridge?"

Rian swung his toy rabbit back and forth. "Well, I don't know if I can help, but I'll try. I know some of the kids and the teachers and the doctors. But I don't know what's in every room or floor. Snowridge is big, but I can only stay on two floors. And the landing area if I'm with Rhydian."

Just the tidbit about multiple floors piqued her interest.

Even if it took five security escorts, Delaney wanted to explore a bit of the clan while Rhydian worked and Rian was in school.

While she didn't want to think the worst could happen, she needed to prepare herself in case it did. Ever since the crowd had devolved into a giant fight at one of her matches years ago, Delaney always looked for escape routes, hiding places, and even multiple exits. It was a habit that had never gone away.

Rhydian would probably never hurt her. However, she didn't know about the others.

She hated being skeptical, but Rian couldn't lose her, too.

And since preparation had always saved her arse in the past, she wasn't going to skip it now.

Chapter Five

Hours later, after finalizing everything with the DDA about Delaney's trial period on Snowridge and attending to the most urgent clan matters, Rhydian sat behind his desk, frowning at two of his most trusted Protectors—Wren and Carys. "You think a gathering introducing the human to everyone would be too dangerous?"

Wren nodded. "You have yet to even introduce Rian to the clan as a whole. Deep down, you know why."

His dragon chimed in. *Why you've put off weeding out the questionable members of the clan, I have no idea.*

Kicking out uncooperative clan members didn't end well for the Scottish clan. I'd like to think we learned from that mistake.

Clan Lochguard in the Scottish Highlands had expelled all members who didn't support their young clan leader, Finlay Stewart. Not long after, the banished members had teamed up with some other dragon enemies and attacked the clan. Rumors said some of the disgruntled dragon-shifters were planning something even worse for the future, although nothing had happened yet.

His beast grunted. *If we don't take care of the problems within our own ranks, then the DDA may never send a group of human females to our clan. And we need a few to come and stay. Otherwise, the clan will slowly die out anyway if there isn't some sort of influx of fresh blood.*

True, it would take about a hundred years for the DNA pool to grow dangerously small, but Clan Snowridge had been around for more than a thousand years. Rhydian wouldn't be the one to encourage Snowridge's extinction. *I'll think on it, but I'll need to be careful and not rush into anything.*

Rhydian returned to the conversation with the Protectors. "We can't keep shielding certain clan members from others. Not only does it create its own kind of division, it'll blow up soon enough and endanger lives. How close are you to finishing your deep background checks on the entire clan?"

Carys replied, "Nearly done. I'll have the list of potential farming candidates to you within the next two weeks."

He nodded. Some of the dragons would be given farms on the outlying edges of Snowridge's land. That way he and the Protectors could keep an eye on them while not having them inside the main stronghold, possibly fomenting trouble and dissent.

Rhydian glanced at Wren. "You at least sent out the clan-wide alert about Delaney?"

The dark-haired male nodded. "Aye, everyone knows she's under your protection. Although we'll see if that ends up being enough because I'm not sure it will be."

Wren had been with Rhydian for years and had even handled the recent purging of certain, disloyal Protectors within Snowridge's ranks. He trusted the male and his honesty. "It'll have to be enough, especially with your team keeping an ear to the ground. And if it isn't, then it'll show us the true colors of some individuals and we can take care of them." He glanced between the pair. "Regardless, keep me updated. If someone so much as makes a verbal threat at the human female, I want to know."

Wren and Carys glanced at each other before looking back at him. Carys spoke first. "You're more protective of her than other guests, even taking into account she's a human. Is there something we should know?"

His beast huffed. *Just tell them. That way, it won't be a surprise.*

They could also try to force it. They've both hinted at how I should take a mate for a while now.

Wren told you about his potential true mate last year. And good thing, too, because she kissed him before he could warn her. Luckily because of him confiding in us, everything was in place to prevent any sort of leadership vacuum inside the Protectors. We should do the same.

Carys stated, "She's your true mate, isn't she?"

Rhydian grunted. "Maybe."

Wren sighed. "That makes things complicated."

"I didn't say I was going to claim her, Wren."

The other male raised his brows. "Why not? This isn't like the last time, Rhydian. You're the one in charge now."

He and Wren were only a few years apart, and the other male had been old enough to witness everything that had happened with Liliwen. "I'm in charge, yes. But that brings its own set of troubles. For now, all that matters is protecting both her and the boy. I hate to be overly dramatic, but our future might just depend on it. After all, if Snowridge can't handle incorporating one human female and a half-human child from outside the clan, then we have no hope of making future human mates welcome."

Carys's mobile beeped, and she checked it quickly before meeting his gaze again. "It looks like Stonefire's head Protector is here."

Rhydian wondered what the Stonefire Protector wanted since he hadn't given Rhydian any sort of notice concerning a visit. "You don't have to be so formal. Kai may not live here, but his mother and sister do. He's family, in a way."

She grunted. "You can say that, but he can be a bit bossy at times, even though this isn't his clan."

Wren jumped in. "Stop it, Carys. He helped us out not that long ago with rescuing the children from the hands of those dragon hunters. That alone puts him in my good book. What else was in your text message? Did his mate come with him, too?"

Carys shook her head. "Not this time. Kai wants to talk to Rhydian alone."

Rhydian's dragon peaked up at that remark. *I wonder why. He almost never wants to speak with us alone.*

There's only one way to find out.

He focused back on the two dragon-shifters. "Bring him here right away, Carys. And Wren? I want you to keep an eye on Delaney and Rian whenever possible. The female's curious, and braver than she should be. I don't want her to cause trouble and sway the clan's opinion of her so early."

Wren stood, and Carys followed suit. The male replied, "Of course. But one last thing—even if you don't intend to take the human as your mate, you still may want to devise a plan in case something happens. Most of the clan respects you, but I don't want to take any chances."

His dragon beamed. *See? Wren agrees with me.*

Ignoring his beast, Rhydian waved a hand in dismissal. "Fine, fine, I'll do that if it'll make you feel better. For now, bring Kai Sutherland here."

The pair left, and Rhydian leaned back in his chair. Coming up with a contingency plan about what to do in case the mate-claim frenzy kicked off was solid advice. However, just the mention of the frenzy made him think about Delaney naked, sweaty, and moaning beneath him.

The vision became clearer, with her long dark hair splayed beneath her as her nails dug into his back. Rhydian reveled in her tight wet pussy gripping him as he claimed her over and over again, branding her with his scent each time he came.

His beast hummed. *Yes, yes. She should be ours. Think of a plan and then let's try to win her.*

Rhydian's resolve to resist the female seemed to lessen by the hour.

However, before he could think of yet another excuse as to why it had to be slow or not at all, someone knocked, and Kai Sutherland walked in.

Thoughts of Delaney would have to wait. Rhydian needed to find out why Stonefire's head Protector was here. Because if Kai were merely here to see his mother and sister, he would've asked for them instead of Rhydian.

So he motioned toward the seat and stated, "Tell me why you're here, Kai."

As the dragonman explained, Rhydian did his best to sit upright and not slouch. His minimal free time was about to get a hell of a lot smaller.

DELANEY ENTERED the main waiting area of Snowridge's school and every pair of eyes inside fixated on her.

Eira—the Protector assigned as her escort for the day—had warned her that coming to the school so soon after arriving would be a bad idea. Mainly because they still didn't know how most of the clan would react to a human in their midst.

However, when Delaney had asked if it was forbidden for her to go the school, Eira had said no. Rhydian had already told the teachers she was Rian's aunt and should be included in the communication chains. And while Rhydian had the ultimate say over any decisions regarding Rian, there was nothing keeping Delaney from seeing her nephew.

And so she'd taken her time walking down the corridors from her rooms to the school area, studying the tapestries on the walls as she went. Given how there had to be many kilometers of tunnels inside the mountain, she had yet to see any bare walls. The sheer amount of tapestries bespoke Snowridge's long history.

But as soon as she'd entered the main waiting area for the school, Delaney had pushed all her questions and thoughts about the tapestries aside. Everyone would size her up, and she wasn't about to let them intimidate her.

So she merely smiled and met each and every gaze inside the room. She had no idea if they were parents, guardians, or other family, but only those with clearance were allowed in this section of the school.

One of the women with blonde hair smiled and rushed forward. She put out a hand. "You must be Delaney."

The woman's Welsh accent meant she had to be a lifetime Snowridge member, or at least from somewhere in Wales. Delaney had no idea if the dragons lived anywhere outside the mountains. That hadn't come up in her research.

Slowly, she took the woman's hand and shook it. "Yes, I am. And you are?"

The older woman—she was probably in her fifties —released her hand and said, "Oh, pardon me. I'm

Lily Owens. My mate is Rhydian's cousin, you see, so we hear any sort of clan news straight away."

Another female in the room sighed. "We all received the same message this morning, Lily. Stop trying to impress her."

Lily glanced over her shoulder at the red-haired female who'd spoken. "There's no need to be snarky, Nerys. I was trying to let her know that we're Rhydian's family, so she has nothing to fear from us." Lily looked back at Delaney. "And my son's mate is a human, too. So I might be able to help you adjust. True, Jane lives on Stonefire—my son is head Protector there—but she visits when she can. And so I have an idea of what you might wish or need to know."

On the surface, Lily seemed genuine. The laugh lines around her eyes and mouth bespoke someone with good humor and who liked to enjoy life.

While Delaney wouldn't fully trust anyone inside Snowridge yet, her gut said this dragonwoman could become an ally.

And if she were to live among the dragons to help raise Rian, she'd need allies. It was best to start collecting them.

Delaney replied, "Thank you, Lily. But I'm still trying to figure it all out at the moment. If I have any questions, I'll ask."

Lily bobbed her head. "Good. And I'll make sure Rhydian gives you all my and Gareth's contact information, too. If you need anything, please call."

She smiled. Lily reminded her a little of her own

mother. "I will." She gestured toward the door where the kids should exit from. "Who're you waiting for?"

"My daughter, Delia. She's sixteen and a troublemaker at times. But she has a good heart, which is what matters."

The same red-haired dragonwoman from earlier—was it Nerys?—chimed in. "Delia's a bit rash, but she has more than a good heart. She saved my nephew from the hunter bastards. If she hadn't gone investigating into his disappearance, along with the others, we might never have found them."

Lily frowned and turned toward the dragonwoman. "Yes, but she nearly lost her dragon in the process. It's a miracle any of them still have their dragons if I'm honest."

Something about Lily's words caused warning bells to ring inside Delaney's head. Rian had been one of the kidnapped children; Eira had told her a little bit about it. Had something happened to him, too?

However, before Delaney could ask for any more details, the younger children filed out of the door first. Rian raced straight for her and stopped a few inches away. She yearned to reach out and hug him, but things were still new between them. So instead, she settled for a smile. "Hello, Rian."

He grinned back at her. "You came, just like you said. Good. Then maybe we can visit the library. I can show you all the books that make dragons look bad. I would like to go exploring, but Rhydian said we couldn't."

Lily jumped in. "It may not be exploring, but you

two should come with me and Delia. I have some freshly baked biscuits. And if we're lucky, Gareth will be home soon and can sing some of those songs you like, Rian. I'm sure your aunt would like them, too."

Rian tugged at Delaney's top. "Can we? Mr. Owens sings well and has some fun songs. And they're much better than the books. The songs have been teaching me heaps about dragons, more than school does."

Lily clicked her tongue. "Now, now, Rian, don't say that. Most of what Gareth sings about are things you'll learn later."

A teenage girl with short, brown hair walked up to them. "Dad's songs *are* better, Mum. I'm older, went through those classes you talked about, and can honestly tell you Dad's music teaches us loads more."

The teenager looked like a younger version of Lily, albeit her hair was brown to Lily's blonde. Even without the introduction, no one could mistake her being Lily's daughter.

Lily placed a hand on her daughter's upper back and pushed gently. "I won't have you disparaging the teachers." She looked back at Delaney. "This is my daughter, Delia. And Delia, this is Delaney Murphy."

The teenager tilted her head and studied Delaney. "The new human. Nice to meet you. I only know my brother's mate—she's a brilliant reporter, which is what I want to be one day, too—and so my knowledge is limited about humans. Maybe I can ask you some questions for the school paper? I'm sure lots of people would be interested to learn more about you."

Delaney blinked. "Um, aye?"

Delia nodded. "And I should record you, too, to make a video. The accent alone will interest my classmates. I've never been to Ireland, even though it's so close. You'll have to tell me all about the places to visit so that when I'm older, I can go."

And before Delaney knew it, she was being herded out of the room by Lily and Delia, listening to a barrage of questions Delia never allowed her to answer and wondering what had just happened.

Eira had warned her about the clan not trusting, or even liking, most humans.

And yet, the Owens were half dragging her for tea and biscuits so that she could listen to some Welsh dragon ballads.

If this experience was what being part of a dragon clan meant, then maybe living with them would be all right. True, she didn't blindly trust everyone and knew there could still be danger lurking. But for the first time since learning about Rian's existence, Delaney thought that maybe her life wouldn't be as isolated inside Snowridge as she'd thought.

Chapter Six

After more hours than he'd wanted to spend, Rhydian had finally finished hashing out the details of helping Kai and Stonefire with a "silent dragon" drug bust.

Apparently, some of the IT people on Stonefire had finally found and hacked the sites used on the dark web for the product. And while Rhydian and Stonefire had only suspected the main business was operating in Wales, Stonefire now had proof.

And so the two clans were teaming up to take down the supplier an hour north of Cardiff. Even though Stonefire had more Protectors and support staff than Rhydian, his people knew Wales much better than them.

Carys, in particular, was a skilled tracker. She would be needed for certain.

The only unease he possessed was not having

enough protection for Delaney if something happened while his people were down south, completing the raid.

His dragon spoke up. *That just means she should live with us until the operation is over.*

Right, because that won't be tense.

It doesn't have to be. If Delaney lets us kiss her, then Rian can stay with the Owens. They would look after him.

No, it's too much of a risk. A kiss would most likely set off the mate-claim frenzy, and with some of my best Protectors down near Cardiff, the clan will be vulnerable.

Stonefire said they'd send some support, and maybe even a few Protectors from Lochguard, too. Bram always has a plan in place.

Bram Moore-Llewelyn was Stonefire's clan leader, one Rhydian wanted to trust implicitly but still hadn't quite reached that point yet. *Delaney is staying down the corridor from us. That's near enough to protect her whilst avoiding temptation.*

His beast paused before adding, *I think she needs to be watched closer. And there might be one other person she could stay with who could do that without me getting jealous—Gwen.*

Gwendolen Price had once been a Protector-in-training. However, during her required stint in the British Army, she'd fallen in love with a human and had become pregnant with his child. The human male had soon after sacrificed himself during a battle to save Gwen. The army had then kicked her out once they'd learned of her pregnancy. Human-dragon relationships had been frowned upon much more five or six years ago compared to the present.

Rhydian sighed. *She's skilled and has continued her self-*

defense training, but it's risky. Gwen rarely comes out of her quarters, unless it's for something related to her daughter.

Well, Gwen has a half-human child, and Delaney wants to help raise her half-human nephew. They have more in common than you think. Besides, we trust Gwen. She's a distant cousin, one we used to play with when we were younger.

His beast was correct. Gwen was slightly younger, and he'd done his fair share of teasing the female when they'd been children.

Just remembering his larger extended family back then, before the epidemic that had killed off most of his family about fifteen years ago, constricted his heart. It hadn't been easy going from a large family to him and Gareth. Even Gwen—who he'd never been close to as they'd gotten older—had distanced herself, too, after what had happened in the army.

His dragon said softly, *It could also help us to reconnect with her. Ever since seeing Dr. Allonby for counseling, Gwen has been less of a recluse. This might be the next step she needs to becoming even closer to whole again.*

Nice to see your ability to guilt-trip has only strengthened with age.

It's not guilt-tripping. It's taking the facts and devising the best solution.

Rhydian's inner dragon had always been his partner. Regardless of how annoying he could be at times, Rhydian was still grateful for the beast. He replied, *Let's talk with Gwen first. We can order Delaney to stay with her if need be. But I won't do it without Gwen agreeing to the plan.*

His beast snorted. *I'm not sure Delaney will like being ordered about.*

Maybe not. But her safety is one of my top priorities. Being clan leader always comes first, even when it comes to potential true mates. I won't allow Rian to lose anyone else close to him.

If you say so.

His dragon then turned his back and settled down for a nap.

Which suited Rhydian fine. He had a lot to do, and his beast could be quite chatty at times.

And the longer it took him to visit Gwen and talk with her—as well as possibly agree on details regarding Delaney staying with her—the longer he'd be away from Rian and the human female.

Even if he had clan priorities to focus on, Delaney had a way of making him forget some of his worries for a short while.

And he desperately wanted to spend a little time with her before diving in to his project with Bram and Stonefire.

So Rhydian picked up his pace and headed toward Gwendolen Price's living quarters. It was time to ask her a favor.

When Gareth Owens finished his latest song, Delaney clapped along with everyone else. The man could sing. Not only that, the ballads he'd composed were magical, telling stories of dragons of old in such a way she had leaned forward in her seat to ensure she caught every word.

Once she and the others in the room stopped clapping, Delaney asked, "Have you ever considered recording and sharing those songs on the internet? I'm sure a lot of people would be interested in seeing and hearing them."

Gareth always had a smile, and it didn't budge as he said, "Not really. Until the last few years, the DDA would swiftly erase any dragon-related videos or music from the internet. And while it's a bit different now, I'd rather just sing for my family."

Rian jumped up. "But Mr. Owens, it's so good. And I learned a lot. Other people would, too, if they heard it."

Gareth shrugged. "Maybe. However, we don't have that sort of equipment anyway, so the point is moot."

Delia raised a hand. "Well, actually, we might."

Gareth frowned at his daughter. "What are you talking about, love?'

Delia debated a second before replying, "Kai gave me a microphone, a camera, and some other equipment soon after I was rescued. I think he felt guilty for missing so many holidays and celebrations over the years, and so he spoiled me a little. I didn't tell you about the gifts because I knew you'd think that meant I'd go investigating again."

Lily clicked her tongue. "You're right, I don't like the temptation that equipment gives you."

Delia took a step closer to her mother. "But, Mum, I only want to use it here. There's a lot of interesting things inside Snowridge, stuff we should record and maybe use someday. Not to mention I promised Kai not to run off on my own again like I did with those dragon hunters. And it's not like I'm going to upset him or he might send someone to watch over me every second of every day."

"That might not be a bad thing, Delia," Lily murmured.

Delia didn't bat an eyelash at her mother's words. "I promise not to run away again. Please believe me, Mum, and don't take the equipment away. I don't know if I want to make documentaries or be a reporter yet, but something along those lines. The things Kai gave me would help me learn a lot before thinking of my future."

As mother and daughter stared at one another, having some sort of nonverbal conversation, Delaney eyed the door to the kitchen. This was clearly a family issue, and she shouldn't be here.

A knock at the front door reverberated inside the room before Delaney could even stand. Gareth frowned at the door and then looked at his mate. "Were you expecting someone?"

His mate shook her head. "No, but let's not keep them waiting."

Lily went to the front door and opened it, revealing a tall man with blond hair. It took a second, but Delaney recognized him from an interview she'd seen before. "You're Kai Sutherland."

The male glanced at her with a raised eyebrow. "And you are?"

She had a feeling he already knew who she was—rumor had it that the dragonman possessed connections everywhere, which probably included Snowridge—but she brushed it off. Standing tall, she replied, "I'm Delaney Murphy, Rian's aunt."

"So you are," he murmured.

Rian ran toward Kai. "Uncle Kai! You're back! I thought you said you wouldn't be back for a long time. Is Auntie Jane here, too? She always has the best games to play."

Kai ruffled the boy's hair. "Sorry, it's just me this time. I didn't think I'd be back so soon, either. But I needed to talk with Rhydian and decided to stop by and say hello before heading home."

Kai glanced to her, and Delaney suspected he'd come to ensure she wasn't a threat to his family.

Not one to do subtle dances when it came to conversations, Delaney walked toward the tall dragon-shifter and said, "So ask me what you wish. That's why you're here, aye?"

"Perhaps."

Lily jumped in. "Kai, be nice. Delaney is our guest."

"But how much do you know about her, Mum?" Kai asked.

Lily replied to her son, "Enough. If you're going to interrogate her, then maybe you should leave."

Kai sighed. "You're too trusting, Mum."

"And you're too suspicious. You know Rhydian wouldn't allow her out and about if he thought she was a threat to us."

Tired of people talking about her as if she weren't there, Delaney said, "It's time for Rian and me to leave anyway. I promised him I'd make dinner and it'll take me some time to find everything in an unfamiliar kitchen." Lily opened her mouth—probably to invite her to dinner—but Delaney beat her to it. "Thank you for the tea and biscuits, Lily. But Rian and I should really be going."

"If you say so, love. But you're welcome anytime."

Kai grunted, but Delaney ignored him. "Come, Rian. You can help me make dinner."

"And Mr. Cottontail, too?"

She smiled, forgetting all about Kai's suspicious nature. "Yes, Mr. Cottontail, too."

"And Rhydian? He needs to eat. We can surprise him."

"We'll see." She took the boy's hand. "Thanks again, Lily, Gareth. And nice to meet you, Delia."

Without another word, Delaney left, her nephew in tow.

While she knew Kai had only been doing his job and thinking about this family, the entire encounter had reminded her of what she faced. A tiny percentage of Snowridge had accepted her, but it wasn't guaranteed that most would.

However, as Rian started trying to sing Gareth's song, making up his own words more often than not, Delaney smiled again. She could put up with it all for Rian's sake. After all, he needed to be around other dragon-shifters to learn and develop his dragon-related skills.

And maybe, just maybe, she had an idea of how to prove to a large group of people that she wasn't a delicate human who could be scared off with a growl or light threat.

Of course it meant sweet-talking Rhydian a little.

Once she succeeded in convincing him of her idea, then Delaney would come out of retirement for one night only. If she held a few boxing matches against some of the other dragon-shifters—most likely Protectors or self-defense trainers—then it would save her a lot of time in the future. Because if she had to stand up to the dragons and show her strength over and over again, for possibly every clan member inside the Welsh clan, it would be exhausting. Not only that, it'd take away her energy for raising Rian.

The trick would be proving to Rhydian she could handle herself, which meant maybe softening him up a little first with a tasty dinner. She doubted there was much difference between human or dragon-shifter men when it came to their stomachs. She'd just have to make the best damn dinner anyone had ever seen. Then when Rhydian was stuffed to the gills and ready to waddle out the door, she could pounce and propose her plan.

Chapter Seven

Rhydian knocked on Delaney's door and did his best to contain his curiosity. The female had invited him to dinner and had hinted at how she had a new event idea for his clan. Since a text message didn't contain a lot of words, it'd been vague. And only because he'd been busy with Gwen earlier had he not pressed for more details.

His beast spoke up. *I like it. We rarely get surprises. Yet another reason she'd be a good mate.*

Not this again.

You said you were open to it. So stop trying to dismiss the topic every time I bring it up.

The door opened, revealing a flushed Delaney wearing an apron.

With bits of her long, dark hair framing her face and the pink on her cheeks matching the sparkle in her eyes, it took his breath away.

Would she ever stop being so bloody beautiful?

His dragon snorted but thankfully remained otherwise silent. Delaney waved him inside. "Come in. Dinner's nearly done."

Rian came racing toward him. And as soon as Rhydian stepped inside the living room, the boy hugged him as he said, "Oh, Rhydian. You're going to like what we did! Me and Auntie Laney did our very best, and even put our heart into the food. Right, Auntie Laney? It was heart?"

She smiled. "Yes, heart and soul."

Her gaze met his and time froze, his heartbeat echoing in his ears.

It would be easy to lean over, tuck her hair behind her ear, and kiss her hello.

And given the heat in her gaze and how her pink cheeks were flushed nearly red, he had a feeling she wouldn't push him away, either.

Then Delaney stepped backward and motioned toward the kitchen and dining area. "I need to check the food or it'll burn. Come. You can join us in the kitchen and set the table."

Rian released Rhydian and clapped his hands. "Yay! Then I don't have to do it. Now I can help you taste everything, Auntie."

Delaney laughed, the sounds like chimes being rung by the wind. "For tonight, yes. But you're going to help with setting the table other nights. It's a very important job, one I hope you'll take seriously next time."

The boy dashed into the kitchen before Delaney could add any stipulations. Rhydian trailed after the human female, doing his best to not watch her hips sway.

Of course the ties of the apron made it almost impossible to do that. It was as if they swished back and forth over her arse to tease him.

His dragon grunted. *She could be ours. Remember that.*

They reached the kitchen and he watched as Delaney stirred something on the cooker. Whatever it was, it smelled fabulous.

Delaney said over her shoulder, "I made Irish stew. I hope you like it."

"I don't think I've ever had it, but I'm not that picky. I usually just snatch something up from the clan's eatery."

She raised her brows. "So you only eat the dragon equivalent of fast food?"

Rhydian growled. "No way. We like real food, not stuff tinkered around with in a lab."

"So does that mean you've never had a proper fish and chips from a shop?"

"We're not exactly near the sea if you couldn't tell," he stated.

Delaney rolled her eyes. "Okay, Mr. Obvious. That didn't answer my question, so I just need to be clearer in the future. Something tells me you constantly pick things apart."

Rhydian spotted the bowls on the counter, moved to them, and picked them up. "It's almost a requirement for a clan leader. When you listen to a dispute between two farmers, or even between two parents over something one of their kids did over the other, you need every advantage you can think of to come up with a fair solution."

Rian sat at the table in the nook and tapped the surface. "Hurry up, Rhydian. I want some stew. My mum always made it, and it was my favorite. I really, really want some again."

While he'd known Delaney was related to Rian, the boy's comment reminded him of how Delaney could bring a little of Rian's mother to life, even with her gone.

His dragon spoke up. *Yet another reason she should stay with us.*

Can't you let it rest for now?

His dragon faked sleeping. At least, for the time being. Who knew how long it'd last.

As Rhydian put one bowl and then another on the table, it struck him how domestic this all was. He'd lived alone for most of his life. Even when Rian had arrived, it'd still been just him and the boy mostly adapting to his bachelor lifestyle of meals from the eatery and finding ways to function without much thought.

However, as Delaney started humming a tune as she turned off the cooker and cut some bread, he wondered how much better life would be if she were his mate.

Not that he'd expect her to do everything. Of course not. But Rhydian would need some help in the cooking department, and he could definitely use some liveliness in his life. Most of the time he didn't think much about living in North Wales inside a mountain or how gray and cold it all could be.

Delaney, on the other hand, could make him forget all about the cold.

His dragon's pretend nap ended and he chimed in. *Go over to her. You don't even have to touch her, but I want to feel her heat and take in her scent. I know you want the same.*

He placed the last bowl and as if of their own volition, his legs carried him right behind Delaney. He murmured, "Can I help you with anything?"

DELANEY COULD FEEL Rhydian's heat behind her.

Even without touching, every inch of her skin was on fire in a good way. If she leaned back, then she could absorb some of his heat and chase away the slight chill that cave-living conditions seemed to cause her.

But if she did that and Rhydian wrapped his arms around her middle, she'd lean back and let him do whatever he wanted with her.

Part of her wanted exactly that. However, the part that constantly thought of Rian pushed it aside. The boy was mere feet away and waiting for his dinner.

A dinner that her own sister had made for him many times over, so much so that it'd become his favorite.

Thinking of her late sister and her nephew banished her awareness with an icy suddenness. Delaney stepped to the side and gestured toward the bread. "You can finish cutting that whilst I get the stew on the table."

She could've sworn Rhydian's finger brushed the top of her arm. However, he was cutting bread with gusto before she could even blink.

If Rhydian was interested in her—and she was fairly certain he was—that could be problematic for her boxing match idea. From everything she'd read about dragon-shifters, they were overly protective of their mates, family, and even clan.

Delaney may not be any of those things—*yet*, a small voice said inside her head—but if Rhydian was as aware of her as she was of him, it could be enough to cloud his rational mind.

Wanting to get both of the men in the room eating and on their way to food comas, Delaney carried the stew pot to the table and set it on the trivet. Rian danced in his seat. "Next time, you need to teach me more about cooking. I want to make stew every day. Stew, stew, stew. Yes, that would be brilliant."

She smiled as she dished it out to Rian's bowl. "If you eat something every day, you'll grow tired of it. Besides, this doesn't have as much veg as a growing boy needs."

"But I'm not a boy, I'm a dragon-shifter. And dragons need heaps and heaps of meat. Right, Rhydian?"

Rhydian chuckled, and Delaney's gaze instantly went to his face. When he smiled, it was as if ten years melted away. Rhydian replied, "Our dragon halves would love nothing more than to have meat all the time, but our human bodies need more. If you want to grow big and strong like Wren or any of the other Protectors, then you most definitely need to eat a lot of vegetables, too."

Rian sighed dramatically. "But I don't *want* to eat them. Most of them taste like dirt."

Delaney was tempted to jump in, but she held back. Something about how Rhydian handled the boy fascinated her.

Rhydian put the breadbasket on the table. "That just means you need to try a new recipe. Lily has some Japanese recipes for spinach and pumpkin that most definitely don't taste like dirt. Maybe she can make that for you."

Rian wrinkled his nose. "Pumpkin? No one eats pumpkin. They're only good for carving faces, like I saw on TV."

"Remember what I said your first week here, about what you need to do with food?" Rhydian asked.

Rian slumped a fraction in his chair. "Try everything at least once. And if I don't hate it, try it again."

"Right. You never know what you truly like until you try things."

Delaney finally decided to jump in. "He's right, Rian. I never would've been a boxer if my dad hadn't made me try a bunch of different sports to find the one I liked."

Rhydian looked at her. "So that's how you became one, then."

She bobbed her head as she slid into her chair.

"Originally, I had wanted to try ballet. But I hated it from the tenth second of my first practice. My dad then had me try all sorts of things, not limiting it to merely ballet or netball, like a lot of other girls. It took years, but by the time I was a teenager, I tried one last thing—boxing—and fell in love with it. If I'd stopped or given up, I never would've found something I loved, something that helped shape who I am today."

As Rhydian stared at her, his pupils flashed to slits and back. What she wouldn't give to hear his dragon's thoughts.

However, before she could ask or say anything else, Rian said, "Well, I want to try this stew. Just to make sure I like it."

She smiled and met the boy's eyes. "Go ahead and eat."

Rian didn't wait for any more encouragement. And as he continued to nearly inhale the contents of his bowl, she surmised he liked it.

Rhydian's sexy voice filled her ears. "This is good, Delaney. I have nothing to compare it to, but I doubt there's any Irish stew better than this one."

His compliment warmed her insides as she watched him overenthusiastically eat his dinner. Between him and Rian, the stew would be gone in a flash.

She should follow suit, enjoy her meal, and move the conversation to something easy. But the longer she kept her idea secret, the heavier it felt in her stomach.

When Rhydian was midchew, she blurted, "The idea I had was to host a boxing match. Me against another female with some degree of training, like one of the Protectors."

To his credit, Rhydian calmly swallowed his food and didn't start choking. His gaze assessed hers. Maybe some would look away at the intensity, but she only matched it.

She needed to prove herself in some way to the clan. And this was all she really could do.

And so she waited to see how the dragon clan leader reacted.

RHYDIAN's first instinct was to say no bloody way. No matter how skilled or strong Delaney may be, dragon-shifters were stronger. Flying, in particular, toned their bodies in ways humans could rarely match.

And yet, hearing how she'd gone through so many activities to find the one thing she loved—boxing— made him resist his first urge.

If someone had tried to tell him he could no longer fly, would he do it?

His beast huffed. *Of course not, unless it would kill us. And even then, we'd have to think about it.*

Careful to keep his tone even, he said, "Most of our female Protectors aren't trained in boxing. In fact, there's only one who has tried it even a little. So your idea probably won't work."

"Then what will? From everything I've heard from Rian, Eira, and even the DDA, most dragon-shifter clans tend to view humans as physically weak and not good for anything but having babies. Strength is held to such a high standard with your kind, and I need to prove I'm not a delicate flower. And I'd rather do it in one go instead of over the course of years and years, having to prove myself to every individual here. I had to do that at the school today, and I didn't like the distrust they showered on me with Rian there. I'm sure he gets similar treatment as there aren't many half-human children here, right? But if I can prove I'm strong all around—both mentally and physically—then it might make things easier for him in the long run, too."

Rhydian hadn't heard any reports about other students mistreating Rian. But he'd been so busy healing the clan after rescuing the children three months ago, it was entirely possible it was happening and Rian had kept it to himself.

Fuck. Had he really overlooked that point so easily? The more he grew to know Delaney, the more he realized how sharing Rian's upbringing would be best for the boy.

Speaking of the lad, Rhydian glanced at Rian to see if he was listening in. However, the boy was happily eating his stew and sharing it with his stuffed rabbit. As long as they kept their voices from being too loud, they should be able to have a quick conversation.

Although he didn't want a quick one, but still, with a child, that would have to be enough until after Rian went to sleep later.

Rhydian leaned over a fraction toward Delaney, trying his best to ignore how her scent grew stronger and made his dragon hum. "I don't know if there's a quick, fix-all solution, Delaney. Humans haven't lived on Snowridge for decades."

His dragon growled. *Of course there's a fairly easy solution. If she were our mate, most people would leave her alone.*

I'm not going to propose that *to her.*

Delaney's voice prevented his dragon from speaking. "What did your dragon say? If what I learned earlier today, about how intricate your dragon halves are when it comes to living life—at least according to Lily—then he should have a say in this conversation, too."

His inner beast raised his head and smugness filled his eyes. Rhydian ignored him. "That may not be the best idea."

Delaney searched his gaze a second before leaning even closer and whispering, "We're going to pause this conversation until Rian is asleep. Then we're going to finish it."

At the firmness in her tone, Rhydian blinked. He'd never met a human with such steel and spine before.

And he rather liked it. No, more than like—he loved it.

He nodded and then Delaney turned toward Rian, chatting about something he didn't quite follow.

His dragon said, *I can't wait for later. You'd better tell her my idea.*

You're crazy.

No, I'm not. It's the most logical and rational solution. And before you say how we can't go into a frenzy anytime soon because of the upcoming operation with Stonefire, that's fine. I can somehow find a way to wait, as long as it's not indefinitely.

Rhydian sensed he would lose this battle, so he tried one last thing. *What about Gwen? She was excited for Delaney to stay with her.*

She still can, until the mating ceremony. Merely putting the word out that Delaney is our mate-to-be will be a good first step in securing her place here.

It was far too soon for any of his dragon's plans, and yet, his beast had a point. And as Wren had said earlier, Rhydian *was* the one in charge now. There would be no uncles or clan leader driving out his female and teaching Rhydian a lesson.

He knew it would bring some troubles, too, but they were issues he should've been working on anyway.

Maybe Delaney was the kick in the arse he'd needed to tackle some of the most difficult tasks he'd ever do as clan leader.

Cleaning out the bad members of his clan wouldn't be easy. Carys and the others had started the process with their background checks, but Rhydian's duty of telling the people they needed to move to one of the farms or to another clan would be much harder.

And yet, as he watched Delaney make a funny face and Rian laugh, he smiled. This could be his family. Yes, it would take a lot of hard choices and hard work, but to come home every day to laughter and maybe one day love could make it all worth it.

Maybe, just maybe, after nearly twenty years he could finally be happy again.

And in that moment, he didn't need his beast

urging or persuading him to suggest it to Delaney later. Rhydian had made his decision and he hoped with everything he had that Delaney would agree to it, too.

DELANEY TOOK one last glance at Rian's sleeping form and gently closed the door.

Her nephew was finally asleep, which meant it was time to pick up her conversation with Rhydian from earlier.

The fact the dragonman had been unusually silent during the rest of the meal—she assumed it'd been unusual, although maybe it was his normal way of being, she had no idea—made her worry a little. He'd turned down her boxing idea. But she suspected his inner dragon had come up with another.

It was time to find out what it was.

Taking a deep breath, she walked down the corridor to the living room.

Rhydian leaned against the mantle of the fireplace. The orange-red glow of the flames danced across his face, making his three scars more prominent.

It was on the tip of her tongue to ask more about them, but that would only delay the important conversation they needed to have.

So she blurted, "Rian's asleep."

He remained leaning but turned his head to meet her gaze. The pupils flashed, looking almost magical in the firelight. "Then we need to have a serious chat, one without any interruptions this time."

She nodded and debated if she should sit or stand. There was no real reason for her to be nervous, yet she hadn't spent much time alone with Rhydian to date.

It wasn't fear making her hesitate, either. Just remembering his heat at her back made her shiver and itch to rush over to him, lower his head, and kiss him.

Dragon-shifters must definitely have some sort of love-inducing powers. That had to be it.

The corner of Rhydian's mouth ticked up. "There's no reason to be nervous. I won't hurt you."

His statement cut through her hesitation and lust-haze. Straightening her shoulders, she replied, "Of course not. I'm trying to decide what the protocol is for talking with a clan leader about important topics. Do I sit? Stand? Twirl and finish with a bow?"

He smiled. "I'd pay good money to see the twirl and bow."

Resisting the urge to give him the double finger salute, she tilted her head and placed a hand on her hip. "Are you going to be helpful or do I have to ring Lily and ask for her advice instead?"

"No, no, don't ring Lily. If you do, she'll be here right away and hover protectively. She may have only just met you, but she has a way about her when it comes to helping those who need it."

"You still haven't told me what I should do," she stated.

Standing up, he took a few steps closer to her. "I'd prefer for us both to stand."

As she glanced up to meet his gaze, she snorted.

"So you can tower over me and try your best to intimidate me?"

"No, because you have too much energy to sit down and stay still."

She blinked. "How do you know that?"

He brushed a section of hair over her shoulder. "You keep tapping your hand against your side and shuffling your feet. And given your former profession, lounging around doesn't really seem your style."

She opened her mouth and closed it again. Rhydian was far more perceptive than she'd given him credit for.

However, as he searched her gaze, she forgot about that and drew on every bit of strength she possessed not to look at his lips. The full lips surrounded by a late-day stubble. A stubble that would rub against her tender flesh and make her wet and needy for him.

Rhydian's voice was husky when he said, "So now that we've established how I'm a master of reading body language, let's talk about earlier when you proposed your boxing match."

"I wouldn't call you a master of body language as it seems to be a recent development. Otherwise, you would've noticed my irritation the first time we met."

He raised his brows. "Do you really want to debate this or talk about what you can do to be more accepted inside the clan, even if only slightly?"

She wanted to needle him for some reason—probably because it was fun—but she managed to keep herself on topic. "Okay, then what's this grand idea of yours?"

"Do you like me, Delaney?"

She frowned. "What are you talking about?"

His finger rose to her cheek and lightly traced it. Her heart rate sped up as heat rushed between her thighs. Rhydian's voice somehow made her hotter as he said, "I think you fancy me, Delaney Murphy. And if that's true, it'll make my suggestion easier."

It was hard for her to concentrate with Rhydian's finger on her cheek and his heat so close. Never would she have pictured him as such a charmer, but she was definitely falling under his spell.

Stupid dragon-shifter powers of seduction. They should be illegal.

"Rhydian, what is all of this about? I don't like beating around the bush, so just tell me straight what you mean."

His pupils flashed, and since this was the first time she'd seen them do so up close, she noticed how they came to sharp points at the top. As they grew round again, the middle fattened out.

They reminded her of cat eyes.

Rhydian replied, "If you agreed to be my mate, then the clan would mostly back off. Not everyone, but enough to make your life easier."

Of all the things she would've guessed, Rhydian proposing that she become his mate hadn't been one of them. "Wait, what? What do you mean agree to be your mate?"

"You wanted to know what my dragon suggested, and that's it. And don't worry, I wouldn't kiss or touch you unless you asked me to."

As Rhydian stared at her with his heated gaze, his pupils flashing rapidly, she doubted him not kissing or touching her would last long. Not because he'd go back on his word, but Delaney didn't think she could maintain a platonic relationship with Rhydian for any period of time.

But to marry him? It was all so sudden.

She didn't want to hurt him, but she needed some clarification. "Say I agree to it." She swore Rhydian growled, but she pressed on. "And it doesn't work out. Is there any sort of dragon divorce? Because if not, then I'll have to find another way to make my stay here easier."

His voice sounded tight to her as he replied, "It's rarer since so many pairings have been, historically, between true mates. However, there is a process for it."

She hadn't even thought about true mates. "Is that why you're so attracted to me? Am I your true mate?"

He didn't hesitate. "I'm fairly sure you are, yes."

To dragon-shifters, finding a true mate was one of the best things that could happen.

However, her sister had been a dragon-shifter's true mate, and it hadn't been happily ever after for her.

That shouldn't matter to Delaney since her situation was completely different. Wales allowed humans and dragons to mate, as well as even live together, unlike back in Ireland.

And yet, she wondered if the Murphy women were cursed when it came to dragon-shifters. It had to be rare that a pair of human sisters both ended up being true mates to dragons.

Rhydian tilted her head back up, to make her meet his gaze. "You're hesitating. You have every right to do so, but I'm curious as to why?"

She didn't have to tell him. From what she'd learned of the Welsh leader, he didn't use fear and pain to make his clan members do his bidding.

However, she'd been sincere earlier when she said she didn't like to beat around the bush. "My sister ended up dead because of being a dragon-shifter's true mate. How do you know that won't happen to me, too?"

His face softened a fraction. "I can't promise you'll never come to harm since dragon-shifters in the UK have some dangerous enemies, namely the Dragon Knights and the dragon hunters." He leaned his head a fraction closer, his gaze turning fierce. "But you will be living within the protection of an entire clan. No, several clans as I have allies in the rest of the UK, too. There is power in numbers, which is something your sister didn't have."

He was right. And on the surface, it was so simple. However, if she was going to even consider the offer, she needed to explore the deeper parts, too. "What about Rian? He clearly cares for you, and if we are pronounced mates, he'll think we're his new family. If it doesn't work out, then he'll be devastated."

Rhydian raised a hand to her cheek and cupped it. The second his skin touched hers, some of her tension faded.

Aye, dragon-shifters must have secret magical powers.

He murmured, "You don't have to answer right this second. Think about it. But know this—I haven't felt such a pull or sense of ease around a female in twenty years. And even compared to back then, that feeling was a fraction of what draws me to you, Delaney. My dragon and I will do almost anything to keep you happy. That's what any mate should do."

The corner of her mouth ticked up. "So if I asked you to do a dance number, you'd do it?"

"I like dancing, so of course."

She blinked. "You like dancing?"

He smiled. "Should I show you?" He took a step back, releasing her cheek, and put out his hand. "Care to dance with me, Miss Murphy?"

Delaney wouldn't say she was a dancer, but she was quick on her feet and a fast learner.

And curse it all, she *wanted* to dance with Rhydian. It was something romantic, almost like out of a movie, and she'd never seen such a thing happen in her thirty years to date. Men just didn't ask ladies to dance out of the blue like that, at least in her circles.

So passing up the chance just wasn't an option for her.

Sliding her hand into his, Delaney nodded. "As long as you teach me as you go, I'd love to dance with you."

His pupils flashed again. "Good. Just remember to let me lead."

She opened her mouth to protest—even though she did have a tendency to take control of situations—when Rhydian turned on some barely audible music.

Placing his phone to the side, he pulled her close and positioned one hand on her waist and readjusted his grip on the one already in his. "On the count of three, we step left. One, two, three."

He moved and she followed. The steps weren't hard, but they took a little bit of concentration.

She focused on not stepping on his feet, and Delaney never noticed how easy it was to move with Rhydian, almost as if they'd danced a hundred times before.

RHYDIAN HADN'T DANCED with a female outside of his clan leader duties, simply because he wanted to, for over a decade.

Part of him had thought he'd be rusty and make a fool out of himself.

And yet, the steps came to him without a thought.

His dragon spoke up. *Because Delaney's our true mate. Moving with her, no matter what we're doing, will always be easy.*

Now who's the romantic one?

You. You're the one who asked her to dance. Not that I'm complaining. It means we get to hold her close and memorize her scent.

Decades of experience told him his beast would soon go down the path of naked images and prodding Rhydian to kiss the human. So he ignored the dragon and said to his human, "You're light on your feet."

Delaney met his gaze, a grin on her face. "Just be

grateful you're seeing it now, and not when I'm trying to punch you and knock you out."

He snorted. "Maybe one day, if you give me a little training, we could have a proper match."

"That would be a tough decision, whether to teach you or not, because if I teach you too well, then I'll lose."

"True, but then I'd keep pushing you to do better."

Her smile faded a fraction. "I can't go as hard as I did even a few years ago. I hurt my knee, and while I can do a match or two for fun as long as I wear a brace, there's no way I could train up and participate in professional matches again."

"You miss them, don't you?"

She shrugged one shoulder. "In a way. I mean, all athletes are on ticking clocks to some degree. Bodies age, and we can't do the same as when we were younger. And I knew one day I just wouldn't be able to keep up with it all." She missed a step but quickly righted herself before adding, "But even if I wanted to practice, I haven't had the time. Over the last few years, I've been taking classes in graphic design, and building up a client base for my new career."

He raised an eyebrow, making sure to turn Delaney at the right moment. "That would require you sitting still all the time. Are you sure that was a wise choice?"

"I've been using a standing desk, which helps. But regardless, there's only so many things I can retrain to do at thirty without spending years and years at university. Graphic design was something I'd always wanted to try anyway, and I'd even built up some regular clients before coming here, so I must be decent at it."

He made the final turn as the music died down. However, he didn't release his hold on Delaney. "Can you still teach boxing without reinjuring yourself? I'm sure some of the Protectors would love the chance to fight against each other, to let off some steam."

She raised her chin a fraction, and Rhydian did his best not to notice her long neck. "Maybe. I've never tried training others before."

"Then maybe give it a go? I can help set everything up as well as put out the invitation. While it's not the same as fighting and competing yourself, you wouldn't have to completely discard that phase of your life. Well, provided you want to do it, of course."

She searched his gaze, remaining silent a few beats. He desperately wanted to know what she was thinking.

She finally bobbed her head. "I'll work on a training plan, although my top priority will still be Rian."

"Of course. I wouldn't expect anything else of you."

She tilted her head, her long, dark hair sliding over her shoulder.

Rhydian wondered what it'd feel like to have her hair brushing his naked chest.

His beast growled, but thankfully Delaney spoke again before his dragon demanded something he couldn't do, such as kiss the female.

She finally replied, "How can you say stuff like that so confidently? You barely know me. Is this all because of the true-mate pull?"

Rhydian answered, "As much as I'm sure some people would love that to be true, no. I've been in charge of Snowridge for about five years now, and I've become rather good at reading people. Between the time spent with you and the background check conducted on you by my Protectors, I have a general framework. And then every additional minute with you fills in the gaps a little more."

Her hand moved from his waist to lay on his chest. Even through the material of his shirt, fire erupted at her touch.

His dragon hummed but didn't say anything. Probably because he was trying to be on his best behavior, as he'd promised he could be.

Delaney stroked her fingers, and Rhydian let out a groan. "You're testing my limits, human, that's for sure."

She pulled her hand away and he wanted to drag it back, but didn't. "I wasn't trying to tease you. To be honest, I wasn't even aware I'd moved my hand. Are you sure you don't have some sort of mind-control powers over me?"

He snorted. "If I did, then we wouldn't be here talking. We'd be doing a different kind of dance in my bed."

Her pupils dilated and he could smell the intensity of her arousal.

Rhydian was getting closer and closer to the edge of his restraint, so he released Delaney and stepped back a few paces. "I'm an honorable male, Delaney Murphy. Even so, I'm getting close to my limit. I'll warn you now that if you kiss me, it'll start off the mate-claim frenzy, which will only end once you're pregnant. And before you possibly say you want it, I can't. Not yet, anyway."

"Why not?"

He loved how she didn't hesitate to find out the reason behind his statement. "There's something in the works, something that's not public knowledge to even most of the clan, and I have to remain in control until it's completed." He paused and added, "And just know that I wish I could tell you more, but I won't violate the promises or trust placed on me. Mates tend to have more privileges, but even then, there are some things clan leaders have to keep secret for a time."

Some females would frown or say that's ridiculous. However, Delaney merely shrugged. "That sounds about right. I mean, it's not as if the prime minister is going to tell his or her partner about a silent strike, or recovery operation, or the like. Well, in some cases, I'm sure. Besides, everyone has boundaries and secrets."

"Between true mates, there aren't many boundaries, though. And some clan leaders confide everything in their mates, and even plan things together."

She tapped her fingers against her thigh. "So if I agree to this true-mate plan, is that what it'll be like between us?"

A small flash of hope flickered inside him. Maybe Delaney would say yes. Or at least it sounded like she was becoming more open to the idea. "Eventually, yes. But I can't share other clans' secrets unless they trust you, too. So we'd just have to convince them of it."

She turned and walked to the far side of the room. "If I say yes, what happens next?"

His beast roared. *She will be ours. Soon, so very soon. It means we need to work hard to finish the operation with Stonefire.*

She still hasn't said yes, yet.

But she will.

He focused back on Delaney. "There would be an announcement. And until the ceremony could be arranged, you'd probably stay with Gwendolen Price, a former Protector trainee with a half-human child."

Delaney's eyes widened. "I thought Rian was the only one on Snowridge."

"Cora—that's Gwen's daughter—is the only other one. But that is a long story, and one that Gwen should tell you, not me."

It took everything he had not to move back to Delaney's side. He needed to end the conversation and say his goodbyes for the night, or he might end up doing something stupid, like kiss the human. So he added, "I can introduce you to her tomorrow. So, will you consider it?"

She bobbed her head. "Aye. I'll have an answer for you in the morning."

His beast grunted. *That's not good enough.*

It'll have to be. Now, shush. He spoke to Delaney. "Then we should probably say goodnight for now."

Delaney's gaze traveled to the door, the one behind which Rian slept. "Will Rian be able to stay with me and Gwen, too, if I say yes? I think it'll be good for him to meet another child like him."

"I don't see why not. We can finalize the details

tomorrow after you have an answer for me." Just for fun, he bowed deeply. "Good night, Miss Murphy."

He expected a snort, but when he raised his head, Rhydian saw the smile on Delaney's face. She replied, "Goodnight, Mr. Griffiths."

She did a quick twirl and exited the room before he even laughed.

Since Eira would be waiting to escort Delaney to her room, he stayed where he was, reliving the dance and ensuing conversation with Delaney.

The evening had made him realize how much he needed the female in his life. And not just for Rian's sake, either.

Rhydian bloody hoped she said yes to his plan. He wasn't sure he could take no for an answer and go back to his lonely, work-focused life.

Chapter Eight

Delaney had spent yet another long, restless night, barely getting any sleep despite the fact she'd decided what she was going to do not long after leaving Rhydian's place.

She wanted to try being mated to him and see how it went.

Mostly for Rian's sake, but also for her own. The dancing the night before, as well as the teasing, had felt more than nice. Not to mention she'd never felt so at ease around someone she'd known for two days.

Hell, she'd had boyfriends for months and months who hadn't been as charming or honest with her. Yes, there was still a lot to learn about him—no one was perfect, after all—but if he'd earned Rian's love already, then Rhydian was probably a keeper. Not to mention the way Lily Owens and her family obviously thought well of him, too.

The hardest part had been putting aside her fear

over what had happened to her sister. She only hoped that Rhydian's words, about him having several clans as allies while her sister had been almost alone, would prove true. Especially if they did go through the frenzy and she birthed a half dragon-shifter child. Because once that happened, she'd never leave Snowridge.

Not that she thought she could do so even without that kind of tie, either. This was where Rian belonged, which meant she did, too.

A knock on the door made her heart jump. It should be Rhydian. To help calm herself, Delaney smoothed her hair and clothes.

Each step she took toward the door made her palms sweat. Why, she had no idea. She'd made her decision.

And yet, the words meant she'd be living with the sexy, romantic, intelligent dragon leader soon, once he finished his important task.

However, being around him but not kissing him until his important task was completed would be the hardest part.

You can keep it in your pants, Delaney. Taking a deep breath, she opened the door.

And promptly let out said breath at Rhydian's tall, lean form standing in front of her.

He'd always been in trousers and a button-up top since she'd arrived, but today he wore jeans and a T-shirt. The casual clothing suited him better, not to mention it revealed his muscled biceps and defined forearms, as well as the edges of his dragon tattoo.

The dark lines and edges made her want to lean over and trace the design with her tongue.

Aye, dragon-shifters were too sexy for their own good.

Delaney must've said it out loud because Rhydian chuckled and said, "Is this yet another power you think we have over humans? That we can make our bodies attractive and drool-worthy?"

"I'm not drooling," she muttered.

"If eyes could drool, yours would be."

She raised an eyebrow. "I'm sure I could make you do the same if I wanted to."

His pupils flashed, and the humor in his gaze was instantly replaced with heat. "Shall we set a time for you to try?"

A small voice inside her head warned that she was entering dangerous territory, but Delaney ignored it. She was going to be this man's wife soon, after all. If she couldn't tease and be herself, then who could she do it with? "How about the first night, once we're mated?"

His pupils changed again. "So you're going to be my mate?"

"I don't see why not? I mean, it works best for Rian."

He growled. "If that's your only reason to saying yes, then I'll rescind my offer."

The stubborn part of her wanted to dig in and say okay, fine, then he could take it back. However, she couldn't let that part of her personality overrule everything in her life. There was more than just her to think about now. "It's not just for Rian's sake. It's for me, too."

He relaxed. "Good, that's the answer I need." He put out a hand. "Then, mate-to-be, shall we talk with Gwen? The sooner everything is finalized, the sooner you can stay with her and start your dragon-shifter training."

She placed her hand in his, the usual spark traveling up her arm at the contact. "What training? As in self-defense?"

He tightened his grip on her hand and guided her down the hall. "For that, I'll have Carys or Eira help you. No, Gwen will help with your clan education. If you want to fit in here and feel accepted, you'll have to learn rather fast, I'm afraid."

"Learn what, exactly? Because if I have to memorize hundreds of names in a matter of days, we might have a problem."

Rhydian shook his head. "Nothing so superficial. However, there are certain clan policies and rules that everyone knows and you'll need to learn, especially since you're not part of the sacrifice program and didn't receive that education from the Department of Dragon Affairs."

She tilted her head. "I had no idea they did that. Little is known of the sacrifice program in Ireland since it hasn't ever been implemented in my lifetime."

"I don't know about other places, but in the UK, sacrifices usually have weeks of lessons and homework. Gwen is probably the best person to help you, apart from me, since she's the only other one I know of for sure who has been involved with a human."

Delaney had forgotten about Rhydian's former

girlfriend, from so many years ago, who had also been human.

Not that she was jealous. However, Lily had hinted about it ending badly. And Delaney wanted to know a little bit about it all while she had the chance. "What happened to you and your human?"

Rhydian missed a step but then continued like before. "Liliwen and I wanted to be mates, but the clan was against it. There was an established anti-human sentiment here at the time, one endorsed by the clan leader, too. And so I was taught a lesson—hence the scars—and she was chased out of the country." His gaze met hers, steel blazing in them. "However, this time I'm in charge. No one will chase you out, Delaney. That I vow."

His confidence made her belly flip. Maybe she was naïve, but she believed him. "I know."

After a few beats, Rhydian nodded. "Good. You believing me is the best thing to happen so far today."

"More than me saying I'd be your mate?"

He grinned. "But I already knew you'd say yes, though. So I count that as something I learned yesterday."

She did roll her eyes at that. "Do all dragon-shifters suffer from being overly cocky and confident?"

"I was right, so it's not really cocky, just observant."

She was about to ask if he was claiming his body-language-reading skills were champion-worthy again, but he stopped them in front of a blue door. Rhydian knocked as he murmured, "This is Gwen's place."

Delaney swore Rhydian had calculated their

position in relation to the destination and timed his responses to it.

However, she forgot all about her wonderings as the door opened to reveal a tall, dark-haired woman. A little girl stood right behind her, her wide, dark brown eyes watching Delaney as if she were some sort of mythical creature.

Rhydian motioned toward Delaney. "Gwen, meet Delaney. And Delaney, this is Gwen and little Cora."

Unlike most children Delaney had interacted with over the years, Cora didn't say anything but rather pressed her face into her mother's side. Gwen smiled down at her daughter. "It's okay, Cora. You know Rhydian, and Delaney is his new friend." Gwen met Delaney's eyes. "She'll warm up soon enough. While she's always shy, she hasn't met many humans over the years, either."

Despite the fact the little girl's father was—or had been—human. And while she didn't know all the details, Delaney was the only human on Snowridge, which meant Cora's father probably wasn't in the picture now, if ever.

In that second, her heart ached for Gwen and her daughter. It didn't matter if one was a human or dragon-shifter, shitty things could—and did—happen without prejudice.

It was Rhydian who spoke next. "Well, with the introductions done, I need to go and take care of some things." He looked at her. "Will you be all right alone here with Gwen and her daughter?"

A small part of her wanted to scream no so that

Rhydian would stay. He was going to be her mate, and she was hungry to know more about him.

And yet, she knew he was a clan leader and he'd always be busy. So she wouldn't be selfish. "I'll be fine. Although I hope I'll see you later?"

He bobbed his head. "Of course. I'll join you at the school later to pick up Rian."

She wondered if it was to let the other parents know he approved of Delaney or because he wanted to see her. Maybe it was both. "Until then."

He finally released her hand, said his goodbyes to Gwen and Cora, and left the way they'd just come.

Gwen's voice filled her ear. "Come in. I'm sure you have questions, and I'll do the best I can to answer them."

Tearing her gaze away from Rhydian's retreating figure, she smiled and entered Gwen's place. Even though she was grateful for the dragonwoman's help and kindness, Delaney silently counted down the minutes until she went to collect Rian from school.

Rhydian somehow managed to leave Delaney's side and focus on his clan for the next six hours.

He'd told Wren, Carys, and Eira about his future mating to Delaney. They'd all been genuinely happy but had also been full of questions.

His dragon spoke up. *I don't know why they kept insinuating that I couldn't control myself.*

Dragons who find their true mates usually aren't patient, and you know that.

His beast huffed. *I don't like being lumped together with everyone else. It took a lot of patience, strength, and intelligence to win the leadership position. They should know better.*

If the trials had included a test involving our true mate, it might have been much more of a challenge for you. But none of that matters now. We need to hurry if we're to make a grand entrance and let all the parents know of our engagement to Delaney.

I hope she doesn't hate the surprise.

Rhydian hoped so, too. If there was one way to get the news out and have it be full of eyewitnesses to his genuine attachment to Delaney, then being a little possessive of his future mate in front of the parents would do the trick. While not everyone loved to gossip, enough of them did to ensure it'd spread throughout the clan within a day or two.

He normally didn't care for gossip, but it would be a lot safer—as well as easier—than having a formal gathering and making Delaney face all of Snowridge at once for the announcement. This way, they should at least get used to the idea first, and then he could remove the highest threats before allowing her to be exposed in the large gathering hall.

His dragon grunted. *I don't like all this waiting and seeing. I want to be direct and tell everyone outright. That way, we'll have her sooner.*

No, ensuring there's less drama and commotion, meaning we can focus on the operation with Stonefire, will make any sort of claiming happen sooner.

Before his dragon could say anything else, Rhydian entered the main waiting area of the school and waved to the parents already there. One of the females—Nerys—came up to him and asked, "Are you picking up Rian again? I was surprised to see the human yesterday."

He raised an eyebrow. "Why? She's his aunt."

"Yes, but…"

The honorable male in him wanted to challenge Nerys for her implication, but the clan leader in him knew he had to be more diplomatic.

At least until he was officially mated, and then everyone knew that to mess with his mate was to poke at both his human and dragon halves.

So he forced a smile and said, "But what, Nerys?"

She glanced to the side and shook her head. Nerys wasn't very high on the dominance scale among the Snowridge clan members. Well, when it came to the males anyway. She seemed to challenge the females every chance she got, causing her fair share of headaches that Rhydian had to smooth over.

His dragon snorted but thankfully remained silent.

Rhydian spoke again. "If I didn't approve of her taking care of the lad, she wouldn't have picked him up yesterday. You should know that, Nerys. I take the clan's security very seriously, especially after what happened with the children not that long ago."

Nerys bobbed her head, murmuring, "I know, Rhydian," and moved to talk with one of her friends.

Rhydian didn't like having to remind people of their place, but sometimes it was necessary. Otherwise some of their dragon halves would become uncontrollable. And if it happened often enough, they could even turn rogue and risk not only other lives in the process, but theirs as well since the DDA handled rogue dragons.

Which sometimes resulted in death.

Pushing aside such thoughts, he mingled with some of the other parents. Rhydian had barely made a few more greetings before he felt Delaney enter the room. Even with his back turned, every inch of his skin came alive, alert to her presence and movements.

Murmuring his pardons to the male dragon-shifter he'd been talking with, Rhydian turned toward Delaney and walked straight to her. Without a word, he took her hand, raised it to his lips, and kissed it.

The warmth of her skin sent heat through his body, but only through years of experience did he keep his cock from responding.

Delaney blinked. "Um, hello."

He raised his gaze and winked. "I wanted to share our secret."

On cue, one of the dragon-shifters in the room asked, "What secret?"

Rhydian stood, pulled Delaney to his side, and answered, "Delaney Murphy has agreed to be my mate."

Nerys blurted, "Why?" at the same time Lily Owens shouted, "That's wonderful!"

Everyone spoke at once, and Delaney whispered into his ear, "What are you doing?"

He replied low enough that only she should be able to hear it. "Garnering you protection."

"And what about Rian? Shouldn't he know first?"

Rhydian had thought long and hard about that detail. "If we want the word spread quickly, this is the best way to do it."

There were questions in Delaney's gaze, but Rhydian didn't have a chance to answer any more of them before Lily was right in front of them. "So when did this happen? Is she your true mate? Or was it that you just couldn't resist her? Not that I can blame you. She's clever and beautiful. You can't go wrong with that package."

Delaney motioned for him to answer. Her movements were a bit stiff, and he had a feeling she was angry.

However, he could handle her anger when they were alone. With Lily Owens on their side, it would go a long way toward getting the clan to accept his human.

Yes, Delaney had already become his. He may have to woo her and win her still, but merely having her at his side relaxed him in a way he hadn't felt in years.

He finally replied, "True mate or not doesn't matter. Which you should know, given what happened with your son."

Lily's son, Kai, was mated to a human who wasn't his true mate. And the pair held a stronger bond than many of the true pairings he'd seen over the years.

Lily never looked away from his gaze. "That doesn't mean I'm not curious."

Delaney spoke up. "I'm his true mate."

Gasps echoed in the room, but Rhydian didn't let them unsettle him. "She's right. But the mating ceremony won't take place just yet. I'll let everyone know when it does."

Delaney muttered, "I hope I'm included in that."

His human was most definitely upset. The question was why. She'd wanted to stop all the dragon-shifters from questioning her at every turn, and his actions would most definitely help with that.

His dragon rumbled but didn't say anything. So Rhydian said, *What, are you against me now, too?*

I'm staying out of it.

At that moment, the kids started filing out for the day. Rhydian didn't release his hold on Delaney as he headed toward Rian. Although he'd have to be completely clueless to not notice how stiffly she walked next to him.

Aye, they would be having a serious talk as soon as possible. He wanted the teasing, warm female from earlier to come back.

Rian rushed toward them. "Rhydian, Auntie Laney, you both came!"

Delaney stepped away and hugged Rian. "We did." She released the boy. "Are you ready to be my helper again tonight?"

Rian shuffled his feet. "I want to, but Osian asked me to go home with him after school for dinner. I promised last week I'd go. And Rhydian said we're supposed to keep our promises."

Delaney squatted down to Rian's eye level. "Don't

worry about it, Rian. Go to your friend's house. We can make something extra special tomorrow, okay?"

Rian lifted his gaze, his eyes bright. "Yes! I can't wait. Maybe I'll go to sleep early so I can wake up early."

Delaney laughed, and Rhydian secretly wished he'd been the one to make her do it.

The human female replied, "You can always try. Now, where's this friend of yours? I'd like to meet him and his parent or guardian."

Rhydian of course already knew Osian's parents and decided Delaney would do best to talk with them by herself.

However, he leaned down and whispered to her, "We'll leave together and go to my office. My schedule is free for at least an hour, so we can talk."

She bobbed her head curtly. Standing, she took Rian's hand and went to meet his friend's mother.

His dragon finally spoke up again. *You fucked up somehow.*

Yes, I gathered that. The question is, how.

You'd better find out. I don't like Delaney this way. She shouldn't be distant.

I agree, dragon, I agree.

As another clan member came up to ask him about something, Rhydian did his best to focus a few more minutes on his clan. He'd have Delaney alone soon enough, and then he'd find out why his human was so upset.

∾

DELANEY WASN'T skilled at showing one emotion when another was churning inside. However, she did her best to smile and be polite with Rian's friend and his friend's mother.

Thankfully the dragonwoman didn't bring up Rhydian's recent announcement. Otherwise, her temper may have burst forth.

As soon as she left Rian with his friend and his mother, Delaney walked back to Rhydian. Regardless of what she wanted to say in that moment, she would save it for when they were alone. Clan politics could be a dangerous thing, as Gwen had explained, and right now Rhydian was in a precarious position. Something about weeding out those who wanted him to fail.

Furious as she may be, she didn't want to risk his or anyone inside Snowridge's lives.

The man was smart enough not to put an arm around her waist, though, as they left. They walked in silence, each step making Delaney's heart thump harder as she clenched her fingers into a fist.

Even though she'd never been inside Rhydian's office yet, she barely paid it a second glance as they entered it. The moment he shut the door, she took a few steps away and turned to face him. "Why did you surprise me with your announcement like that? You should've told me first."

"I didn't think it'd be a huge deal. You consented to be my mate, and so I shared the news."

She growled. "Is this how it's to be, then? You make the decisions and I just passively sit by and accept them? Because that's shite, and you know it."

He frowned. "Of course not. I just want the clan to be more accepting of you a little bit before I push their boundaries further."

In some corner of her mind, the rational portion, Delaney would acknowledge Rhydian knew how to best deal with his clan.

However, something that had happened to her years ago, during her early professional boxing days, kicked that rational tidbit to the side. "I want to be an equal, Rhydian. I blindly followed a man once before, deferring to his experience, and it nearly cost me everything."

The slight irritation from Rhydian's face vanished. "What happened?"

Delaney paced, clenching and unclenching her fingers. Just remembering the bastard made her want to punch a wall, not caring if it'd break her hand.

Calm down and tell him. Taking a deep breath, she continued pacing as she blurted, "I had a fucking manipulative bastard as my first boxing manager. And I vowed I'd never follow someone blindly again, thinking they alone could decide what was best for my future."

Rhydian's voice was low and gentle as he asked, "What did he do?"

Images flashed inside her mind, bringing up that bastard's face. Just remembering Martin's cocky expression and authoritative tone made her stop in her tracks, close her eyes, and try to calm the hell down.

After a few seconds of rhythmic breathing, she opened her eyes and faced Rhydian again. She wasn't a coward. "Even though I was new to the professional circuit, I kept getting brilliant matches thrown my way. Names you've probably never heard of, but in my world at the time, were the heroes we all looked up to.

"It all seemed too good to be true and, in the end, it was. A few months after all the brilliant match pairings began, my manager took me to a hotel, walked me to the door of a room, and told me I had to pay my debt and that the man we owed was inside waiting for me."

She swore she heard Rhydian growl, but Delaney knew if she didn't keep going, she wouldn't get it all out without either screaming or bursting into tears. So she added, "I, of course, asked what the bloody hell he was talking about. Apparently the fucker had negotiated the best matches in exchange for me sleeping with the man responsible for setting them up. He never asked me, didn't think I had a place to object, and traded me like nothing more than a choice piece of meat."

She heard the anger in Rhydian's voice when he asked, "What did you do?"

"I wasn't going to whore myself out like that. However, I did walk into the room to tell the arsehole I wasn't going to sleep with him and that I would go to the papers in the morning if he so much as tried to block me from fighting ever again. Even though we both knew I'd be the one to suffer in the end, it was enough. Because there had been a scandal within the Irish Boxing Association not long before, and even a whiff of another scandal meant he'd be fired."

Maybe she should've shared how terrified she'd been during the confrontation, but didn't think she could.

So she continued, "From the next day, I had to start over from the bottom rungs, winning and advancing with my own skill. And eventually, I made it to the top again, all without any arsehole's brand of help."

Delaney stopped pacing and stared at the ground. She hadn't told anyone about it all before, not even her sister since Rosaleen had run off with the dragon-shifter before Delaney had been ready to share her story.

It had taken her a long time to trust anyone again. And even though she knew she'd won in the end, winning a championship without the promise of having to sleep with anyone to do it, it still affected how she acted.

Torn between crying and wanting to be alone to sort out all her feelings, she didn't notice Rhydian take a step closer until his gentle voice reached her ears. "I'm sorry, Delaney. I had no idea. Tell me there's a way for me to prove I'm not like that bastard from your past."

Rhydian's words helped, but she knew her experience would taint her relationship for a while yet.

The best she could do was to suggest, "Talk to me, okay? I want to make decisions together because I never want to be in a relationship—professional or romantic—where someone decides my fate for me. I can't do that again. I know you're clan leader and if it comes to safety, I recognize that you know what's best in most cases. But even so, talk to me, convince me it's the best pathway. Can you do that?"

She finally met his gaze again and waited to see

what he said. Because Rhydian's answer would determine so much about her future, one she thought she'd known but could now change in an instant.

BOTH THE HUMAN and dragon halves of Rhydian wanted to find the fucking arsehole who'd hurt Delaney and teach him a thing or two about treating people with respect.

While he may make decisions for others at times inside his clan, he'd never barter someone's body or soul so easily, let alone for his own personal gain.

His dragon roared. *He should die for hurting her. She's our mate and ours to protect.*

Those words reminded him of how difficult it would be to rein in their protective instincts.

But for Delaney, he would try his hardest. She was worth it, and so much more.

Then she asked him if he would talk with her about decisions. After a few beats, he answered, "I will always try. I wish I could say yes, I'll always consult you, but sometimes there are split-second decisions when danger is involved. If hunters invaded the clan, for example, I would do whatever it took to protect you. However, there wouldn't be time to discuss it. For everyday things, I will. But I can't promise for everything, Delaney. Can you accept that?"

As she stared at him, Rhydian resisted the urge to pace. He had no idea why her answer meant so much to him. He'd known her a matter of days.

And yet, it fucking mattered. He wanted her, but he also wanted to lead his people to a better future. Not just for him or for some sort of posterity. No, children such as Rian deserved a safe, stable existence.

The only question was whether he could have both without making Delaney miserable.

His beast hissed. *We wouldn't make her miserable. She will be treasured, consulted, protected, and so much more.*

That's not enough in some cases, dragon.

Delaney turned toward him, standing a little straighter. "What about for the mate announcement going forward? Will you consult me on that? As well as how we get the clan on our side?"

He noticed she hadn't answered his question, but put it aside for the moment. Hope dangled in front of him, and he was going to try seizing it. "We can work together on that from here on out, I promise you. If you want a clan gathering, even after I lay out all the pros and cons, we'll do it. If you want to send a formal clan-wide email, we can do that, too. If you want to make me dance in front of the whole clan, holding you close to show how much I want you as my mate, I'll do it. But I can't promise I can do that sort of thing with everything that happens."

The corner of her mouth ticked up, and relief washed over him. Maybe hope would soon turn into reality after all.

She said, "I like the dancing idea. Beyond the fact I like dancing with you, I think it'll have a more lasting effect than someone merely reading words on a screen."

He risked a step closer, but the smile didn't fade from Delaney's face. He nodded. "Then we'll dance. Five times if need be."

"Maybe not that often. Although I know a thing or two about putting on a good show. Maybe we can work together and have a more informal gathering, with dancing and even some theatrics?"

Rhydian had never tried acting or entertaining for any role outside of being clan leader, but if Delaney had some ideas, he'd try his best to put on the show she wanted.

And while he wanted to keep talking about details with Delaney, maybe even make her laugh in the process, he couldn't ignore her lack of an answer to his question. Because her answer would determine everything. "And my truth about sometimes making decisions without you?"

She tilted her head. "I can't say I like it, but compromises should happen both ways, and I can't expect for you to be the only one to concede. I do think talking more will help, especially as we learn more about each other and the respective worlds we come from."

He put out a hand, palm up. "Then shall we dance to seal our deal? Us both sharing more with each other, learning one another, to try to make this work?"

His dragon murmured, *I want to know her better in* all *ways.*

Delaney slipped her hand into his, her skin against his washing away the lingering doubt. She replied,

"Teach me a few new dances, Rhydian. After all, we need to find the perfect one to show off to the clan."

He slowly pulled her close, loving how she fit perfectly in his arms. "And once you have the hang of the steps, we can talk some more, too. Maybe we can each take turns asking a question? No limits, just honesty?"

She smiled up at him. "I'd like that. Although I hope since I bared my soul a wee while ago, I get to ask the first one?"

He pressed a little more against her waist. "Of course, love. Ask me anything."

And so they danced and talked about small things, each of them trying to get to know the other without tearing up old wounds.

Rhydian definitely owed her more of his past as well, but he'd wait for the right time. After all, one gut-wrenching story a day should be the limit. Besides, as Delaney smiled and teased him, allowing him to guide her through the dance, he was a tad selfish. This, right here, was what he wanted. A future with a brilliant, brave female who wouldn't be his subordinate, but his equal.

He'd just have to work hard at making sure he could keep her and eventually claim her as he wanted.

Chapter Nine

The next morning, Delaney stared at the blank ceiling of her bedroom and couldn't help but smile. What had initially started as one of her worst fears—for a man to try and manage her like in the past—had ended up being one of the best nights of her life.

And she hadn't even kissed Rhydian, let alone had sex with him yet.

Still, her previous dating life had been spotty, infrequent, and had never been one-tenth as romantic.

Maybe romantic movies weren't as completely bullshit as she'd always thought before. She'd just been around the wrong kind of men. For all she knew, all dragon-shifters were that way.

A pounding noise emanated from outside her bedroom, probably from the front door.

If something had truly been wrong with Rian, Rhydian would've shouted or made more noise.

However, it was just a few barely audible thumps, which made it all the more strange.

Frowning, Delaney got out of bed and walked to the door. By the time she reached it, the pounding had stopped.

She muttered, "Who the hell would be knocking so early in the morning?"

That's when she noticed the folded paper on the floor.

Picking it up, she unfolded it and read: *Check the outside of your door.*

The words made the hair on the back of her neck stand up. With no signature or any sign of who wrote it, Delaney knew she'd have to be cautious. Which meant she wasn't bloody opening the door until someone she mostly trusted arrived.

Rushing back into the bedroom, she picked up her phone and dialed Rhydian. He picked up on the second ring. "Delaney? What is it?"

She didn't waste time with any pleasantries. "Someone left a creepy note under my door. Can you come and make sure it's safe? I don't want to open it, in case there's a booby trap or something there."

He growled. "I'll be right there. And don't open that door until you hear me say it's okay to do so."

The line went silent and Delaney clicked off her phone. Looking back at the note lying on the table, she realized she'd made a mistake in picking it up. For all she knew, it could be covered in some sort of powdered substance to make her sick or even kill her.

For the first time since arriving on Snowridge,

Rhydian's words about how some dragon-shifters didn't like humans finally sunk in.

The thought of being able to have a party, dance, and endear clan members to her side all seemed like a dream now. Even if it worked for most of the clan, there would still be those who wanted to harm her, no matter what Rhydian said or even if he mated her. After all, the timing of the threat so close after Rhydian announced taking her as his mate couldn't be a coincidence.

Maybe she'd be looking over her shoulder for the rest of her life if she stayed. Much like how her sister had done, until the day she'd died.

Before her mind went down the road of what else could go wrong if she stayed, there was a knocking and Rhydian's voice came through the door, albeit a bit muffled. "Delaney, I'm coming in. Is that all right?"

Relief flooded her body at his voice. Moving back toward the door, she undid the chain and unlocked it. "Come in."

She retreated as the door opened. She noted the fury in Rhydian's eyes for a second before she looked at the door.

Written in red paint were the words, *Go home, human bitch.*

Rhydian's low voice filled her ear, "Are you okay, Delaney?"

Seeing his face again helped to ease her fear a fraction and help reason return to her brain. Taking a deep breath, she nodded and decided humor was her best coping mechanism at the moment. "I've received a few worse threats over the years. I just didn't expect one so soon. It must be some kind of record, aye?"

Rhydian growled. "Whoever did this knew what they were doing. With you as my future mate, this is a challenge to me more than you."

She studied his face a few seconds as he shut the door. His scars almost seemed starker against his skin. Combined with the fury in his gaze and his clenched jaw, he would intimidate quite a few people.

However, Delaney remembered him teasing and dancing with her. The anger wasn't at her, and if she was to stay on Snowridge—and yes, she was going to stay, seeing Rhydian's face again had banished her rash panic—she needed to calm him a little and maybe even find a way to help him.

The years of Rhydian Griffiths handling the problems of his clan alone were over if she had anything to say about it. Together, they might be able to make the clan safe enough for her to never have doubts about staying on Snowridge again.

Delaney gently placed a hand on his arm and lightly stroked his bicep with her thumb. As his muscles relaxed under her touch, she asked, "So what do we do about this?"

He frowned. "This is my problem, not yours, love."

"Why is it only your problem when it concerns me too?" He opened his mouth, but she continued before he could say anything. "Aye, you know the clan better. However, there are many ways people can help one another. Just talking about your ideas or frustrations with me could clear your mind of anger. That way, you can handle it more rationally than in your current state." She stroked his arm again. "After all, I was having doubts of being able to stay here until you arrived, reminding me that I don't have to face these things alone. You don't have to, either, Rhydian."

Rhydian's pupils turned to slits for a few beats before growing round again. He replied, "My dragon seems to agree with you."

She smiled. "You having two personalities in one body will come in handy for me winning arguments in the future."

Rhydian's face didn't lighten at all, which worried her. Had he been hiding just how much some of his clan hated humans?

He ran a hand through his short, dark hair. "I want to pretend this isn't a massive problem, but it is, Delaney. My plan to quietly weed out the clan and send most of the troublemakers to the outlying farms won't work now. Because I'm sure someone has seen this, or at the very least the culprit took pictures and is bragging to likeminded folk, encouraging others to help them drive you out for good. And in the process, maybe even take me down as well."

She leaned a little closer. "Then change tactics. Plans are all well and good, but when it comes to life, you need to be able to pivot or adjust in a second. So now, rather than being upset about the road being hard, we need to accept it and find a way to conquer the fucking thing."

The corner of his mouth ticked up. "You're too bloody marvelous, you know that?"

She shrugged, ignoring how his words warmed her heart. "I had to learn that lesson or I never would've survived beyond my first boxing match. Because if I had only stuck to my predetermined plan, then it meant someone punching me and maybe even breaking my nose. And call me vain, but the fewer times my nose is broken, the better."

Rhydian finally smiled, turning his head to better display his scars and pointed to them. "I lost my vanity long ago." Before she could reply, he took her hand and squeezed it. "So I'm overly cautious and you're a bit vain. There. Neither one of us is perfect. However, together, maybe we can be a little bit more so." He gestured toward the door. "Tell me everything that happened up to you reading the note, and then I'll call a few of my top Protectors here. Together maybe we can devise a plan. And since you'll have to be a part of it, no matter how much I don't like you being the focus of anyone's hatred, you most definitely will have a say in the matter."

Delaney had wondered if Rhydian's promise the night before, about including her when possible, had been genuine. But in this moment, he proved it would be.

Which only made her want to fight harder for her right to stay on Snowridge.

And so, as she explained every detail from her first knock to the letter, her split-second uncertainty about staying earlier was forgotten. Maybe alone she would've had problems, but with Rhydian at her side, they could face anything. She was almost certain of that now.

RHYDIAN QUESTIONED Delaney about every little detail, but as soon as she voiced concern over the letter being covered in some sort of harmful substance, he rushed her to the surgery and had her tested for them. Even though Dr. Maelon Perry was expediting the test results as much as possible, it was still taking too bloody long.

Especially since the doctor had placed Delaney into a temporary quarantine, away from him.

And he didn't like it.

The only positive thing was that Rian was still staying at his friend's house, completely unaware of the threat, and so Rhydian didn't have to worry the lad unnecessarily.

Of course, it made him miss Delaney all the more. Somehow the female had become an integral part of his life, and it was emptier without knowing he could see her, touch her, dance with her whenever he wanted.

He readjusted on the sofa, and then again, trying his best not to get up and pace.

His dragon spoke up. *I want to be with her, too. But if we don't follow the doctor's orders, he'll send us out of the surgery until he's ready to invite us back. And that will only put us farther away from our female.*

Dragon-shifter doctors were the only ones who sometimes had authority over clan leaders. Rhydian didn't always like it, but he knew his friend only had everyone's best interest at heart. *And Maelon would bar us from the surgery until Delaney is released, too.*

Then let's do as much work as we can whilst we wait. That will help distract us.

Right, because you're going to be able to concentrate and not think about Delaney?

His dragon huffed. *I'm going to try. I've already restrained myself for days and haven't kissed her.* His beast paused and added, *One way to maybe speed things up would be to ask Stonefire for help.*

I want to say yes, but doing that could be seen as a sign of weakness, both from within the clan and from Stonefire's side.

Why would it be, though? Not only does the majority of our clan want an alliance with the other British dragon clans, Stonefire asked us for help not that long ago, when they needed to talk to one of the retired doctors here.

That wasn't really a favor, and you know it. Communication between clans shouldn't be so hard. Besides, we still need to help with their upcoming operation so we can pay back our debt for rescuing the children. Asking yet again for assistance would put us back to owing them, and I don't want that.

Aren't they our allies? The point of having allies is to have someone else at your back, ready to help if need be.

Rhydian didn't reply right away. Ideally, that should be the case. However, no one living could remember a time when the dragon clans in the UK had asked one another for help without strings attached, jumping up to assist simply because another clan needed it.

True, Stonefire and the Scottish clan, Lochguard, were growing ever closer to that scenario. But those two clans had had lots of inter-matings between them, which made their close alliance natural. Snowridge, on the other hand, had very few inter-clan matings.

Although he, as well as the other UK leaders, hoped to change that eventually.

There were whispers of a plan to bring a large number of dragon clans together to talk and hopefully make treaties or alliances. However, that was nothing more than an idea at the moment. In the present, Rhydian still needed to be strategic when it came to relying on the help of other clans.

Especially now, when some inside Snowridge were willing to defy him so openly.

Finally agreeing with his dragon about needing a distraction, Rhydian opened his laptop and did some busywork. From experience, he knew that if he did something menial or tedious, it often allowed certain parts of his brain to work on refining the ideas he, Delaney, and his Protectors had thrown about earlier.

Hours flew by as he answered emails, filled out DDA paperwork, and other administrative duties. When the battery on his computer was nearly dead, Maelon finally entered the private waiting room. Rhydian quickly closed his laptop, stood, and asked, "How is she?"

"She seems to be fine. Preliminary tests came back negative. However, I want to keep her here for a few more days, just to be certain." Maelon paused a second to adjust his lab coat before adding, "But if I were a betting male, I'd say the person who wrote that note either didn't think of poisoning her or didn't want to."

The difference between the two scenarios was huge.

Focusing on the doctor for now, Rhydian said, "The Protectors will remain outside her room until she's discharged, Maelon. As much as I trust you, I don't want to risk her life if I can help it."

The doctor nodded, his gaze off to the side, which wasn't out of the norm. "Of course. But she wants to talk with you before you rush off to do anything else. Although given how you've been here the whole time, I don't think you'll be rushing away if you can help it."

He growled. "She's my future mate. Of course I'm going to wait for her."

Maelon raised an eyebrow. "And this sort of behavior will end up encouraging the dissenters. I've seen firsthand when someone accidentally kisses their true mate and how hard it can be to fight your inner dragon's instincts. But sometimes we have to fight them in order to do our jobs well. If you only think of protecting her, it might not end well, Rhydian. I'm telling you this as your friend."

The other mated pairs inside Snowridge saw their other halves all the time, whereas Rhydian was still getting to know his future mate. Staying away from Delaney was a lot bloody harder because of it.

However, Rhydian wasn't going to be petty and bring that up. "Take me to Delaney. After I talk with her, I'll think about what comes next."

Maelon glanced at him a second before looking away again. "I'll start by saying I do like her, Rhydian. But the human female staying long-term will cause problems. I hope you have enough fight in you to ride it out."

From anyone else, Rhydian would bark that of course he did.

However, Maelon was more than a doctor—he was his friend and sometimes confidant. There was something about the male that made everyone want to chat with him, probably because Maelon would rather listen than talk himself. That worked to his advantage as a doctor. "I'm not backing down like when I was younger. I want her as my mate, and I'll do what it takes to ensure it happens. And it's not just for me, either. The clan as a whole needs to be more accepting of humans. Otherwise, we won't last."

"I know." Maelon opened the door. "Come. I'll take you to Delaney and give you a few minutes of privacy before I lay down the rules for you both about how we're going to proceed until she's discharged."

At the steel in the doctor's voice, Rhydian merely followed him down the corridor to the quarantine section of the surgery. Maelon was one of his trusted circle, and Rhydian would save his anger and frustration for those who threatened his mate and not waste it on his friend.

Chapter Ten

It was three long days before Delaney was allowed out of the surgery.

Three days of not seeing Rian, not being able to explain things to him, or to even hug him.

The only positive was that she'd had a lot of free time to work on some design projects and read. One of the teachers had brought a tablet filled with as many of the dragon-shifter-related books as she could find, to help Delaney get up to speed with their history, customs, and how inner dragons worked.

While some might think receiving homework wasn't exciting, it was more than merely a willingness of the teacher to share information. Rhydian, and at least some of the others, wanted Delaney to fit in as much as possible. And given how humans rarely received so much information so quickly from dragon-shifters, it definitely encouraged her to keep fighting.

However, once she signed her release form and met Rhydian in a private waiting room, the anger in his gaze made her blink. "Now what's wrong?"

Since they were alone in a most likely secured room, he didn't hesitate to reply, "Rian is having trouble at school, to the point I have to keep him from going to class for a while."

She resisted the urge to clench her fingers into a fist. "What happened?"

"Some of the children are calling him names, pushing him around, and trying to make him unhappy. Thank fuck for his cheery disposition, although I do wonder how he's hurting inside."

"All because of me," Delaney murmured as she glanced to the ground.

Rhydian closed the distance and gently took her chin between his fingers, raising her gaze to meet his. "I'm sure it would've happened with or without you—it might've been happening all along. Besides, Gwen's daughter has had her fair share of bullying, too, and she isn't old enough to even attend school. It's the parents' fault and no one else's. If they don't condone the bullying, then they should be doing something about it."

She remembered something she read and didn't hesitate to say, "Maybe it's just a matter of exposure and the lack of it. Could you invite some of the older, adult dragon-shifters from Stonefire or Lochguard who are half human? The children wouldn't pick on them, and it would show they are just as much dragons as the full-blooded ones."

"That may work." He moved his hand to her cheek and lightly caressed it. "Where did you come up with that idea?"

She did her best to ignore how her heart soared at his praise. "I had a lot of time to read over the last three days, and there was a mention about how clans had done it before. There was a time when the now-defunct Scottish clan near Stirling had tried to bring human mates into their fold but had met some resistance. Lochguard had suggested they bring some of their own human mates and half-human clan members." She shrugged. "The book said it worked. Or, at least it kept them around for another hundred years or so before they eventually were disbanded and scattered mostly between Stonefire and Lochguard."

Rhydian studied her a few beats before replying, "You're a dangerous combination, Delaney Murphy. Beautiful *and* clever."

The corner of her mouth ticked up. "And stubborn. You most definitely forgot stubborn."

He laughed, and some of the strain from the last few days melted away. More than ever, she wanted to stay on Snowridge and get to know this dragonman. Not just because it felt right, either. Her reading had genuinely made her interested in dragon-shifter policy and changing Snowridge. Information had provided the spark she needed to truly care about the future of the Welsh clan.

But first, she needed to figure where she fit into it all. "As much as I'd like to talk about how wonderful I am, reality is just outside that door, Rhydian. Once I see Rian again and give him the biggest hug, what happens next?"

Rhydian gently stroked her cheek with his finger as he said, "You'll be staying with me until this is all sorted. Don't worry, I'll keep you in a separate room as not even I want to tempt my beast with you beside me. But fewer people will try to scare you, or worse, if you're in my home."

Trying not to think about how hard it would be to sleep a room away from Rhydian and not think about him, she nodded. "Okay, as long as your home doesn't become my prison."

"I'll try my best not to make it one. Although until things are calmer, you will always have security near or with you."

She sighed. "I had a feeling you'd say that."

He pulled her close, moving a hand to her lower back. "It'll get better soon, love. And not just with Rian and hopefully using your idea of inviting half-human dragons here, either. Wren, Carys, and I are putting things into motion as we speak."

She tilted her head. "How?"

He shook his head. "I don't want to discuss it here, just in case someone's listening. But just know that we've been busy. " Rhydian moved one hand down and switched on some music on his phone before moving his mouth to her ear. She had to strain to hear him as he added, "I know who vandalized your door and left that note, as well as all his compatriots. They will be transferred from this clan soon enough, at the DDA's discretion."

Delaney moved her face to look at him again and blinked, careful to keep her voice low so others most likely couldn't hear her. "I thought you didn't like relying on the DDA for those sorts of things?"

Rhydian grimaced as his pupils flashed at the same time. Like before, he moved his mouth to her ear. "I don't. However, it's easier to have the perpetrators on the DDA's radar so that we don't have a rebellion of rogue dragon-shifters, like what happened with the Scottish clan."

"When will all this be done?" she asked in a hushed tone.

His breath danced against her ear again as he replied, "Within the week. Soon after that, we'll have that gathering so I can show you off as my future mate."

She searched his eyes. "Surely it can't be that easy to clean up the clan? Otherwise you would've done it before I ever set foot on Snowridge."

He grunted. "My pride got in the way before. I wanted to solve the problem singlehandedly, not daring to ask anyone for help. But now there's you and Rian to consider. And I'll take all the help I can get if it means securing you two as my family."

Her heart melted a fraction. "Rhydian."

"It's true. Even with the worry and anger, and even frustration over the last three days, I want you here. I care for you, love. And that's far more important than trying to be some sort of all-powerful savior."

She cupped his cheek and stared into his eyes. While Delaney wanted to smile, sigh, and lean against her dragonman, the last three days had given her a lot of time to think and acknowledge reality. So she said, "This is going to become a battle that lasts for years to come, isn't it?"

Rhydian moved his head a fraction closer, his hot breath dancing on her face. "Maybe. But what happened to your fighting spirit, love? Are you sure you're feeling all right? Should I have the doctor look at you again?"

"No, no. I'm fine. Just tired, and a wee bit frustrated at being cooped up."

He raised an eyebrow. "Is that all?"

Damn the man. He knew her too well despite their short time together. His powers of perception definitely had to be a dragon-shifter thing. "Well, reading about the history between dragon-shifters and humans made me realize how long this fight has been going on. If it were just me, then I'd stay here and fight with everything I have and remain at your side. However, there's Rian to think about." She paused, not wanting to say the next few sentences, but she knew she had to. She finally continued, "I can be stubborn, and full of ideas, and so much more, but it should come down to what's best for him, aye? Would he be better off living alone with you?"

Rhydian's pupils flashed and he growled. "Of course not. These problems have been here a long time, and it's not your fault."

"Are you sure, though? I rushed everything and made a mess of it."

"Look, I was dragging my arse at cleaning up the clan. But you gave me a reason to do my duty and take care of it. If anything, you're helping Snowridge, Delaney, even if it doesn't feel like it quite yet. Not to mention it's obvious how much Rian needs you, too."

There was only sincerity in Rhydian's gaze. Oh, how she wanted this dragonman as her own. And yet, she couldn't quite jump wholeheartedly into the idea without running through all the options. "I want to believe you, but then I keep thinking about how my sister kept her distance to protect me. Sometimes, to do the best for the ones we care for, we have to stay away."

He leaned down until his lips were a few inches from hers. With his hot breath dancing against her skin and his scent invading her senses, it was hard to not close the distance and kiss the man.

His husky voice filled her ears. "But in this case, the best thing is for you to stay. Rian adores you, and I don't want you to go, love. And not just because you keep invading my dreams, making me want you more than anything, either. You are the link to securing Snowridge's future because if my clan can't accept you, they won't accept potential human mates, either. And it's only so long until the clan becomes extinct."

A fraction of the weight on her shoulders lifted. "So I'm a sort of trial run?"

The corner of his lips ticked up. "Yes, you are." He leaned his forehead against hers, making her gasp at his heat. He added, "For the clan, at least. To me, you're anything but. I can't imagine you not being here,

Delaney. You make my world brighter, not to mention less lonely. Maybe it's a bit selfish of me to ask, but won't you stay? For me, for Rian, for everything Snowridge could become?"

She smiled. "No pressure, huh?"

He caressed her cheek and she leaned into the touch. "I have other ways of convincing you to stay, if you only have the patience to wait. There are benefits to being a dragon's true mate, after all."

She snorted, remembering something she'd read. "You mean how your semen gives me an orgasm?"

His eyes flashed. "Yes, but that's the lazy male's way. My dragon and I agree that you should always come before us, and then when I do, too, it'll be just a bonus."

Maybe with another bloke, the words would be corny and she'd roll her eyes. But Rhydian's teasing helped to wipe away her doubts about staying. Not completely, but at least a little. Enough to tease him back. "Unless you want a challenge. Maybe make me come twice the first time before you do?"

He growled. "I wish I could say yes, but I've been thinking of you all the time these last three days and I'm not going to last as long as I like the first time, love."

She chuckled. "I guess even dragon-shifters have faults."

He pulled her up against him, her entire front pressed against his, making her gasp at the heat of his body. Rhydian leaned over to her ear and lightly bit her earlobe before saying, "Everyone has faults, but I assure you, sex between you and me won't be one of them."

At the certainty in his voice, Delaney shivered. "You have too much power over me already. Maybe it's a good thing we can't have sex right now."

His hand moved from her waist down to her arse. As he rocked her against him, his hard length pressed into her belly, sending fire between her legs. "I want you more than anything, Delaney Murphy. But since I can't, believe me when I say I'll have lots of fantasies to fulfill by the time I can."

Her earlier worries were forgotten. Her entire being ached to feel Rhydian's skin against hers, his mouth devouring her as he thrust his cock inside her.

He whispered, "I'd start by nibbling my way down to your breasts, drawing your hard nipple between my teeth before teasing and suckling you until you beg for my cock."

She dug her nails into his back, aware they were in dangerous territory and yet, she couldn't stop from asking, "And then?"

"Then I'd continue my way down, spreading your legs wide and admiring your sweet pussy. I'd watch as you grew even wetter for me before I finally leaned down and lapped your sweet honey."

Delaney rubbed her lower body against his, needing the friction against her clit. "And next?"

"Next, I'd move to your hard little bud, licking and lightly biting until you scream and come apart at my touch. I'd never stop my torture as you orgasm, doing my best to draw it out and drive you mad."

She was nearly rocking against Rhydian, but she didn't care. "You'd better not stop there."

"Oh, there's no fucking way. I'd strip, position my cock, and thrust to the hilt. Once you were used to my size, I'd claim you over and over again, thrusting hard and deep until you were nearly ready to come again. Then I'll pinch that hard clit between my fingers and revel in your pussy milking my cock. Only once you were coming down would I finally let go and make you orgasm all over again."

Delaney was so close, if only she could get a little more pressure against her clit.

Rhydian murmured, "Let me help you, love. I can at least give you this right now."

If she had any rational thought left, Delaney might've paused and wondered if it was a good idea to let Rhydian finger her before they'd even kissed.

And yet she was too far gone and nodded. "Please. I'm nearly there."

He moved her away a few inches, undid the button and fly of her jeans, and then slowly slid his hand inside her pants.

The instant his rough finger touched her pussy, she moaned and arched toward him. "Even if it's just your finger, I want you inside me. Now."

He didn't hesitate and slowly entered her. Clinging to his arms, she moved her hips to hurry him up. "More, give me more."

With a growl, Rhydian removed his finger and thrust back in with two. He continued the movement, hitting the secret spot inside of her that made her even hotter.

By this point, Delaney panted. And Rhydian had only used his fingers.

Damn, she looked forward to what he could do with his dick.

Then Rhydian lightly brushed her clit with his thumb, and she could do nothing but ride his fingers and hold on. Soon the pressure built and she crested over the edge, her pussy squeezing Rhydian's fingers as he continued to move.

By the time she finally came down, she was slumped against Rhydian's chest, grateful for the support or her knees might've gone out.

Rhydian's voice rumbled under her ear. "And that, my dear Irish lady, is merely the tip of the iceberg of what I want to do with you."

Rubbing his chest in slow circles with one of her hands, she said, "I have a few fantasies of my own I'd like to try." She ran her hand down to the hard outline of his cock against his jeans. "I can show you a peek of them right now."

Hissing, Rhydian grabbed her hand and pulled it away. "As much as I want to say fuck yes, I can't, love. It's too dangerous. No matter how honorable me or my dragon might be, it could make our resolve snap and start the frenzy."

Doing her best to hide her disappointment—she knew it had to be this way, but she still didn't like it—she asked, "When will this operation of yours be over?"

"If I have any say in the matter, less than two weeks."

She looked up and did a double take at his pupils rapidly flashing between round and slitted. The question she'd been about to ask faded. "Are you okay?"

His eyes finally stopped changing and the pupils remained round. "I will be. I just need to let you go and put some distance between us."

She stepped back and was grateful she could stand upright on her own again. "Not for long, I hope?"

"Not if I can help it." He gestured toward her pants. "Tidy up and then we'll go. Rian's waiting for us at home. I explained as much as I could to him, but he'll have questions. I hope you're ready for them."

As she made herself presentable again, she smiled at the word home. There would be plenty of fights ahead. But now, Delaney had sorted through most of her doubts and was determined to come out the winner.

She bobbed her head. "I think so. I plan to be honest more than anything. I hope that matches your parenting style."

Rhydian snorted. "If winging it by the seat of your pants is your style, too, then yes."

She grinned and met his gaze again. "As it happens, yes, that's it. Although at some point, we'll need to talk more about what we both expect."

"Of course." He reached out a hand and she placed hers in his without hesitation. "Now, let's go. It's time to face the clan and the future."

Together, they left the surgery and headed toward Rhydian's place. Wait, no, their place.

Aye, their place. Together, they would defend their home and show everyone that humans and half humans belonged on Snowridge like anyone else.

Chapter Eleven

If someone had told Rhydian even a few months ago that he'd be standing in the main landing area, waiting for some dragon-shifters from Lochguard and Stonefire to arrive to help his adopted son, he would've called them mad.

And yet, here he was, waiting for some half-human dragons, as well as even a human- and dragon-mated couple, to come and interact with the children for a special day at school.

His dragon spoke up. *We probably should've done this a year or two ago, once Stonefire started changing things in the UK.*

Given how restrictive the DDA was even two years ago about dragons from one clan interacting with another, it probably couldn't have happened. The approval process to officially let us meet would've taken months, not days.

A few dragons appeared in the distance. Rhydian glanced at Wren and his head Protector nodded. Those were the Stonefire dragons.

He and Wren remained at the edges as a familiar golden dragon landed first. It was Kai Sutherland. The male had barely touched the ground before his wings shrunk into his back, his limbs grew smaller, and his snout morphed into a human nose and face.

Kai waved hello, but then focused on the black dragon who hovered in the air. He carried a basket in his rear talons and gently laid it on the ground.

Kai went to the basket and took one and then another toddler into his arms before a woman most every dragon-shifter in the UK would recognize on sight exited it, too.

Melanie Hall-MacLeod was here.

Rhydian had been against the celebrity-like human coming, but Delaney had convinced him that she would be the best human to visit precisely because everyone knew who she was. They may still be trying to scare away Delaney, but Melanie had not only Stonefire but the entire Department of Dragon Affairs office behind her. Not to mention the media as well. The children would think twice before blurting out a hurtful comment.

Or so they hoped.

His beast chimed in again. *She'll be safe. Kai wouldn't have brought Melanie here if he hadn't thought so, too.*

Still, if anything happens to her or her children, it could destroy our fragile alliance.

Have faith. The worst offenders are already on the farms and being monitored by the DDA.

Melanie took her son back from Kai and headed toward Rhydian, a smile on her face. Many people had underestimated the human female early on because of her kindness and shorter stature.

She reached Rhydian and rearranged her grip on her son, who was trying his best to lean backward. Probably to be let down, from what little Rhydian knew about a toddler's behavior. Melanie nodded at him. "Hello, Rhydian. While I'd like to run through all the formalities, if we don't find somewhere for Jack to run around, it might not end well. While Annabel loves flying in the basket, Jack hates the small space."

Rhydian resisted blinking. He'd never really held a conversation with Melanie before, and it was hard to believe this female talking about her children's habits was such a force behind changing things for dragon-shifters in the UK.

As he tried to think of where he could take them so the kids could play, Melanie's mate had shifted to his human form and strode over. Tristan MacLeod, daughter on his hip, placed a possessive arm around his mate's waist. "Rhydian."

"Tristan."

The dragonman was content to stand there in silence. Rhydian knew Tristan was a teacher. No doubt the male had his students in line without more than a blink.

Thankfully Kai came over to break up the awkward silence, and Rhydian turned his attention to the dragonman and asked, "Aren't there supposed to be a few more coming?"

Kai answered, "Sebastian will be here soon. He's waiting to help escort the Lochguard dragons in."

Rhydian frowned. "Why?"

Kai shrugged. "Let's just say that the father of the twin girls is overprotective. And most definitely not a Protector, so it was the compromise we struck with Lochguard to allow them to come."

Rhydian had heard of the mysterious female twins born not that long ago. "Whilst I understand the dramatics the half-human twin females will bring, is it safe for them to come here? They're only babies."

Melanie did her best to keep her son from falling as she replied, "Their mother wants to help. Not only is she human, but she's one of the toughest nurses you'll meet. She shouldn't have trouble with the kids."

Tristan muttered, "Her mate should've stayed home. The students will eat him alive."

For a second, Rhydian realized the divide between his clan and the two others.

His beast spoke up. *Give it time. They've cultivated their alliance and friendship over a couple of years.*

Kai spoke up again. "Which is why not only our Protector is waiting to escort them, Lochguard sent their second-in-command, too. Both of the male Protectors are half human, by the way. So both children and adults can interact with your students."

Neither Stonefire nor Lochguard had been sure they could send one of the few half-human adults or not. Many of the half-human members were parents, builders, nurses, small-business owners, and the like. While everyone here today could easily stand up to some skepticism and being tested, not everyone could. It didn't make them any less valuable to the clan as a whole. It took all sorts to make a clan healthy and happy.

His dragon grunted. *Which maybe now we can focus more on since the worst offenders are out of the mountains.*

Hush. We'll talk more about that later.

Rhydian gestured toward the door. "Kai can take you and your children out of the cold, Melanie. I'm sure his mother can find somewhere for the twins to play until the presentation at the school."

Jack moved to lean sideways, and Melanie sighed. "I hate to miss the others' arrival, but it's probably for the best. We'll see you soon, Rhydian."

The female's warm smile was contagious and his own lips turned upward.

Once the family of four and Kai were gone, Rhydian waited with Wren for the others and asked, "Have you met the other Protectors coming?"

"Not since the clan leader trials down south, for Clan Skyhunter. But if Lochguard is allowing the twin females to come here, then their leader must trust them."

In dragon-shifter lore, twin females were a sign of change and forthcoming peace. They were incredibly rare among his kind to begin with since dragon-shifter populations skewed male. On top of that, he hadn't ever heard of a human and dragon-shifter pairing producing a set of female twins before, either.

His beast said, *It'll be good for the students. After all, if a pair of half-human female twins are supposed to bring peace and prosperity, they may start to see mixed children in a different light.*

I hope so. Rian wants more than anything to go back to school.

Even though it'd only been a week, the boy hated being at home. Rhydian and Delaney had learned just how close he'd become to his friend Osian, as well as most of the teachers. Given the recent upheaval in the boy's life, he deserved stability again.

Several more dragons came into view and Rhydian focused on them. He'd been forewarned about Fraser MacKenzie—the father of the twin girls—and he needed to try and be courteous and not rise to the bait.

DELANEY STOOD outside the school's auditorium with Rian at her side and smiled down at her nephew. "Are you ready?"

He bobbed his head. "Yes. Rhydian taught me how to look brave, even if I'm a little nervous."

It twisted her heart to think such a young boy had to learn such a lesson so soon, but hopefully today would change things to the better not only for Rian but her, too. "And just remember, there are loads of other half dragon-shifters in there. You'll get to meet them before any of the other students come in."

Rian tugged her hand. "Let's go, Auntie Laney. I want to meet them."

Taking a deep breath, she opened the door and guided Rian inside.

In the middle of the big room stood a much larger group of people than she'd thought would attend.

Some she recognized from articles and news reports she'd seen online—such as Melanie Hall-MacLeod—but the others were unfamiliar.

However, she didn't have long to catalogue the different people before a little girl who probably wasn't even yet two walked over and wrapped her chubby arms around Delaney's leg.

She smiled. "Hello, little darling, who are you?"

"Bell. Me Bell."

An American woman's voice filled her ears. "Good job, Annabel." Delaney then met the gaze of Melanie, and the woman continued, "You must be Delaney." Melanie looked down at Rian. "And you're Rian, aren't you?"

Rian tilted his head. "You talk weird, like in the cartoons."

Melanie laughed. "Yes, my accent does stick out here. But I hope we can still be friends?"

Rian studied Melanie a second, and it pained Delaney to know the boy was more careful than many his age.

He finally bobbed his head. "I think so. Rhydian said you were great. And human, too. Like my mam was."

Melanie's gaze turned sympathetic. "I'm sorry about your mom, Rian. But from what I hear, Rhydian and your aunt love you very much."

Even though she and Melanie had just met, Delaney's eyes teared up a little. The other woman had no reason to try and help Rian, and yet here she was, doing so.

It seemed the rumors about Melanie Hall-MacLeod having a huge heart were true.

A Scottish male's voice drifted from behind Melanie. "So here's the wee lad then." A tall, ginger-haired bloke carrying a baby—the man had to be Fraser MacKenzie according to the descriptions she'd received—moved next to Melanie before crouching down. "I hear you haven't met many half dragon-shifter children to date. Come say hello to my daughter, Skye. She's just like you—half human and half dragon-shifter."

Rian leaned over and stared at the sleeping baby. "Are you sure she's part dragon? She looks like any other baby to me."

Fraser scrutinized Rian's face. "And you look like any other boy to me."

Rian stood tall. "My dad was a dragon, and so am I."

Rhydian had long ago explained to Delaney about how no one knew if Rian's dragon would awaken or not, given his captivity months ago.

However, Delaney had hope and was ready to defend her nephew when Fraser nodded solemnly. "You already act like one, lad. You'll do fine." He lowered his voice. "Who knows, maybe one day Lochguard will try to get you to come to Scotland."

Rian leaned against her side and she wrapped an arm around his shoulders. Rian murmured, "I like it here."

Melanie—who had managed to get her daughter into her arms again—said, "And so you do. It just means we'll have to visit again, so you can be the older, protective friend to our babies."

Rian made a face at baby Skye. "She's so little. I don't think she'd be fun to play with."

Fraser laughed. "She basically eats and poops right now. But one day, lad, that will change." He lowered his voice. "And let's hope my mate doesn't add you to her list of potential mates for our daughters. I swear she's going to weed through everyone old enough before their second birthdays."

A Scottish woman's voice carried over. "I heard that, Fraser."

"And it's true, aye?"

The brown-haired woman she was pretty sure was Holly if she was Fraser's mate answered, "Maybe. But I'm not the only one with plans for Summer and Skye. Shall we tell them your ideas?"

"They're good ones, honey. You agreed earlier."

"I wouldn't say agree…" the other woman drawled.

Not wanting an argument to break out right before the other students came in, Delaney jumped in. "Who wants to introduce Rian to all the other visitors?"

Melanie put out a hand. "Will you come with me, Rian? That way your auntie can meet some of the other adults and probably ask boring adult things."

It was true Delaney had wanted to talk to Holly in particular—she was a human mated to a dragon-shifter and had suffered her fair share of danger because of it —but only if Rian was okay with it.

He glanced up at her. "Will you be okay, Auntie Laney?"

From the moment she'd read her sister's letter, asking for her to look after Rian, Delaney had loved her nephew. However, as each day passed, she learned more about him and loved him even more. Him merely asking if she were okay made her heart fill with happiness. She didn't know how she could ever live without him going forward. "I'll be fine, lad. Go have fun with the other kids and talk with the Protectors."

After her nephew hugged her, he took Melanie's hand. The other woman guided him to the visiting children and the two half-human Protectors.

As soon as they joined the group, the brown-haired woman handed off her baby to Kai and walked over. She smiled. "Hello, Delaney. I'm Holly. I heard you had some questions for me?"

So she'd been correct—this was Fraser's human mate.

Fraser, still standing nearby, mumbled, "I swear you know everything."

She grinned. "Good you recognize that, Fraser. It'll make things easier."

As the couple stared at each other with grins, Delaney longed for the same.

She and Rhydian were definitely more comfortable with each other, but the mate-claim frenzy—or lack of one—laid between them. She had a feeling that until it was completed, she couldn't really grow as close to Rhydian as she wanted.

Let alone admit she was falling for him.

Not wanting to go down that path and risk the Scottish couple guessing her thoughts, she cleared her throat, garnering both of their attention. "If possible, I'd like to talk with Holly alone."

Fraser readjusted his grip on his daughter. "Aye, I suppose you do. I think I need to go over there and prod Tristan a little anyway. His sister Arabella asked me to, and I better keep that promise."

He walked away with a wink and Delaney frowned at Holly. "I don't know how you keep up with who is who so easily."

Holly shrugged. "I don't remember everyone's names, but Arabella is the mate of Lochguard's clan leader. So it's probably best you learn that one."

She liked how the other woman was straightforward. "I will, then. And I hope you'll answer the rest of my questions just as directly."

Holly smiled. "I'm not sure I could answer them any other way, Delaney. Too many years as a nurse, aye? And I still work as one part-time on Lochguard."

Holly bringing up she was a nurse was actually perfect. Because one question hung above her more than any other. "That means you know about the risks for humans who birth half dragon-shifter children. There's talk of a treatment to give me a better chance of survival. Is that something I can do here?"

Reaching out a hand to touch Delaney's bicep, Holly bobbed her head. "Aye, of course you can. All you need are regular shots of dragon-shifter's blood. Preferably from the father of your child, or one of his family. I suspect Rhydian won't hesitate."

"Do you know him then?"

"Och, not really. But he told Lochguard's leader

that you're his true mate—as a precaution and a warning, you ken—and while there are some bad true mates out there, I don't think Rhydian is one of them."

"No, he's not," she murmured with a smile as she remembered him attempting to make breakfast for her earlier in the morning. And in the end had served her burnt toast with a rubbery fried egg.

"Your smile tells me heaps, Delaney. You should be fine."

Delaney lowered her voice, hoping none of the dragon-shifters could hear. "I want to be, but there's still a lot of danger lurking around simply because I'm here."

Holly grimaced. "Aye, I know. And I'm not a stranger to it, either. Someone kidnapped me, after all, and caused me to lose my first bairn."

"I'm so sorry."

Holly waved a hand. "It can't be undone. And at least I have my daughters now, which helps."

The woman in front of her was strong indeed.

And while Delaney didn't want to be insensitive, she had another question burning in her belly. Hoping Holly wouldn't be offended by her directness, Delaney leaned forward a few centimeters and asked, "Was it all worth it?"

Holly glanced over at her mate, holding up one of their babies. "Aye, it was. Fraser is what I didn't know I needed. Meeting him made my dad happy, too, in the long run." Holly met her gaze again and sighed. "The only drawback is the bloody legend surrounding my bairns. I don't want them growing up with ideas of grandeur."

Finally, Delaney could offer to assist someone else. "Well, if you ever need help grounding them, let me know. I think the humans in the dragon clans are the ones who can treat them more normal than the dragon-shifters. On top of that, I can even teach them a few boxing tricks when they're older. That way, they can drive off any threats or strangely obsessed believers of the legends."

"I'll have to take you up on your offer, for both treating them like any other children and for the boxing. And maybe, once I'm a wee bit fitter from birthing the twins, you can teach me, too. We humans can always use a few tricks to keep our mates in line."

Delaney laughed. "Anytime. If your mate will allow it."

Holly shrugged. "He won't object. And if he does, then I'll appeal to his dragon half. He'll want me to be as safe as possible."

Delaney didn't miss the opportunity to ask, "So do you have any tips for me on how to handle a dragonman?"

Holly leaned even closer and whispered, "Once this event is over, we can escape for a cup of tea and I'll tell you most of what you need to know."

As she and Holly laughed over their respective dragonman's grunting habits, Delaney felt a little more weight lift off her shoulders. While she'd enjoyed talking with Gwen, Lily, and the other dragon-shifters who had tried to welcome her, she realized now how she'd needed to talk with another human in the same situation as her. Not only to help sate her curiosity, but it gave Delaney reassurance that her fate wouldn't end up like her sister's.

RHYDIAN HALF LISTENED to the visiting guest speakers as they took questions from the students and answered them.

While the children had been hesitant at first, the more Melanie and the others talked with them, the more open they'd become.

Maybe this was what his clan had needed.

His dragon spoke up. *We should have a stronger alliance after this. And not only that, Delaney has made a friend.*

The two human females sat to the side, listening attentively to the speakers. However, they'd both been chatting earlier and Delaney had laughed quite a few times, too. He replied, *I only wish she had another human inside Snowridge to befriend.*

Soon. If things keep progressing this well, we can ask the DDA to send some humans here to possibly find a mate.

Rhydian hoped so. Although as he stared at Delaney's profile, he wanted to claim his own mate first. And not just with a ceremony, either. He wanted to go through with the frenzy.

The presenters finished their talk, and when the teacher asked the students to give them a round of applause, almost every child did so.

He noted the few who didn't. Rhydian didn't want

to keep a list of possibly problematic children, but for Rian's sake, he had to.

Once the students had all filed out—Rian included since he'd asked earlier to go back to class and Rhydian had agreed—he made his way over to the group from Stonefire and Lochguard. He didn't waste time finding Kai, motioning with his head for the Protector to follow. Once they reached the far side of the room, Rhydian asked in hushed tones, "Do you have a few minutes to talk about our project before leaving?"

Kai grunted. "I promised my mother I'd take everyone to her place. But once I do that, we can talk."

"Good. If Delaney can go with you to Lily's, then I'll be in my office finishing a few minor things for the plan."

"Of course. I'll escort her to my mother's."

With that, Kai headed back toward the group and Rhydian went to Delaney.

As soon as he reached her, Holly smiled and left them alone. He murmured, "Can I pull you closer and hold you for a few seconds before you go with them?"

Delaney placed her hands on his waist and closed the distance between them. "Does your dragon need to do a little claiming in front of everyone?"

"While he always wants that, it's for me. I couldn't stop staring and noticing how beautiful you are."

Running her hand up his back, she lightly stroked as she replied, "I would kiss you right now if I could." She glanced over her shoulder at the other group and back again. "I hope with Kai here you'll figure out exactly when I can do that."

His dragon growled. *Tomorrow, if I have any say in the matter.*

I wish, dragon, but it'll be a few more days than that.

He focused back on his mate-to-be. "Me, too, love." He leaned over to nuzzle her cheek, inhaling her lovely scent of summer and sunshine. "But since we can't, if Rian can stay at his friend's house for dinner, we can at least have a few hours alone. Although I won't be eating much food when something much tastier is right in front of me."

She lightly slapped his back. "Rhydian, stop. They can probably hear you."

He leaned back to meet her gaze. Relief flooded him when he saw she wasn't angry. He was slowly learning what he could do, while she was also slowly learning to trust him and realize he wasn't her former bastard manager. "All of them are either mated or wishing they were. What I just said is tame compared to what many other dragon-shifters would say about their females. I'll save the dirtiest for when we're alone."

The corner of her mouth ticked up. "I can't wait to hear the non-tame version of Rhydian Griffiths."

He brushed a section of her hair back from her face. "You'll definitely meet him when my dragon half comes out during the frenzy. I'll never be able to outdo him in that department." He paused and quickly whispered, "You're not afraid of him, are you?"

She hugged him tighter against her. "He's a part of you, so of course not."

"What I wouldn't give to kiss you right now, love."

As they stared into one another's eyes, his heart

raced as his body heated. Rhydian hadn't wanted someone so much it hurt for nearly two decades. While it hadn't been all that long, he no longer could imagine a life without Delaney at his side.

His dragon grunted. *We do whatever it takes to keep her. She's our mate. She belongs with us.*

Only when a whistle came sailing through the air, combined with a "Don't worry, we've shielded the bairns' eyes from the free show" from Fraser did it break the spell.

He sighed at the same time Delaney giggled. Turning his head over his shoulder, he growled, "Mind your own business, MacKenzie."

"Why? You wanted to get to know us better, and this is who I am. Most learn to love it. And if you're not one of them, I'll just pretend you are."

Tristan sighed. "Can we visit Kai's mother now? The more annoying MacKenzie brother should behave better in front of her."

Rhydian reluctantly released Delaney. "Go ahead. But if you drive Lily mental, then I'll have a chat with your leader, MacKenzie."

He swore he heard "Good luck with that," from Fraser. But Delaney's voice quickly banished the thought from his mind. "Come find me when you're done. I learned some things from Holly, and I have some questions."

"Of course, love." He dared to kiss her cheek, lingering to taste the saltiness of her skin before adding, "I'm glad you've made a friend."

"Me, too."

Kai barked they were leaving. The male was definitely too familiar to do so to Rhydian, but they were heading out before he could do more than blink.

His dragon spoke up. *I like them being here. I hope we can have more visitors soon.*

In a strange way, Rhydian did, too. *Let's focus on the operation with Stonefire and claiming Delaney first. Then we'll think about a gathering of some sort with other clan members attending.*

And to help reach that point quicker, he left and walked to his office. He had a lot of administrative duties to tackle before he could talk with Kai, let alone with Delaney, too.

Chapter Twelve

A few days later, Delaney was checking her chicken pie in the oven when Rian yelped from the living room.

After closing the oven door, she raced into the room to find him sitting on the floor with his head to his knees, his hands over his ears. Dropping to his side, she asked, "What's wrong, Rian?"

"I—"

He stopped and leaned against her, curling more into himself.

Oh, no. Something was definitely wrong.

And while she needed to call Rhydian, she couldn't do so until she made sure Rian was okay.

Gently stroking his arm, she asked, "Does it hurt?"

"No." He grunted a few times before falling silent.

The silence cut through her heart. She'd tried her best to learn what a dragon-shifter child needed, but it clearly hadn't been enough. He needed a dragon-shifter's help.

Before she could think of how to get it, Rian sat up and growled. After a few more minutes of him shaking his head while keeping his eyes tightly shut, he finally dropped his hands and opened his eyes.

His dazed look only made her heart beat faster and her stomach churn. However, Delaney did her best to keep her voice calm as she asked, "What happened, Rian? Are you all right now?"

Before he could answer, his pupils turned to slits and stayed that way.

She drew in a breath. Had his dragon finally come out and spoken with him?

It should make her happy since many people had thought he would never have an inner dragon presence. However, no one knew if Rian's dragon would be normal or not after his time with the dragon hunters.

If Rian's dragon didn't act right because of the medical experiments everyone thought the hunters had performed on him, she would work even harder to find a way to help the other dragons take down the bastards.

No. She wouldn't think of how things could go south. Delaney needed to be positive right now, for Rian's sake. His dragon had to be okay. He just had to. She'd only just found her nephew and couldn't bear the thought of losing him forever.

And not just because of her sister's pleading, either. Rian was her son now. She loved him with everything she had, and Delaney would do whatever she could to help him.

Focusing on Rian, she kept her voice even as she asked, "Did your dragon start talking with you, Rian? Did he finally come out to play?"

It took a few beats, but his pupils became round once more. The boy visibly slumped, as if his dragon had sapped all his energy. "Yes and no. He's hungry. And loud. And keeps roaring."

Her belly churned even more. Maybe the doctors and Rhydian had been right—something *was* wrong with Rian's beast. "Does he threaten you? Or say bad things, such as wanting to hurt people?"

Rian's eyes changed again. What she wouldn't give to be able to hear what was going on inside his brain.

She eyed her mobile phone in the kitchen. Could she leave long enough to get it and not upset Rian or his dragon? Because Delaney was running out of options and recognized that Rhydian would have a better idea of how to handle the situation.

Then the boy spoke again, his voice halting. "Food. I want food. Lots of food."

The strange changing of his tone tipped her off. It was like when Rhydian let his dragon take control to talk with her. She just needed to placate Rian's dragon a little, distract him with something to eat, and then she could contact Rhydian.

Gesturing toward the kitchen, she replied, "I have dinner just about ready. There's plenty, too, and you can eat as much as you want."

"No waiting. Food. Now."

"I can fetch you a snack." She put out a hand. "Come on. Let's go to the kitchen."

Rian's pupils remained slitted as she stood and guided him to the kitchen. His movements jerked a little, and she only hoped it was because his dragon wasn't used to being in control.

Rhydian had laid out some worst-case scenarios, but she refused to believe they'd come true. Especially the most awful, which meant his dragon was insane and would never relinquish control.

No. Delaney refused to imagine her sweet, energetic nephew would disappear forever. Maybe Snowridge's doctor would think of something. Or, he could even contact some of the other dragon doctors. Somebody had to have an idea somewhere.

As soon as she had Rian at the table, she quickly took out some crisps and sweets. While not what she'd usually serve right before dinner, she hoped one of them would distract the dragon.

However, in his altered voice, Rian grunted and said, "No. Meat. I want meat."

Since dinner was still cooking, she took out some sliced ham from the refrigerator. As soon as she put it on a plate and served it, Rian started devouring it piece by piece.

Knowing her time was limited, she scooped up her phone and sent Rhydian a quick text message. As much as she wanted to hear Rhydian's voice and have him reassure her everything would be okay, she couldn't risk Rian's dragon listening in.

A quick reply arrived: *I'm coming now.*

Forcing herself to keep a smile on her face, she continued feeding Rian ham and then some cheese—which he seemed to find okay, too—as she waited for Rhydian.

She only hoped he could convince Rian's dragon to let the human half take control again. Otherwise, she'd lose Rian forever, just like she'd lost her sister and her parents.

RHYDIAN RAN down the corridors toward his home, avoiding people and shouting apologies as he went. All that mattered was reaching Delaney and Rian as soon as possible.

Because Rian's dragon had finally come out and taken control.

While the dragon could be normal and only be wanting some time out after years of being stuck inside Rian's brain, the boy's beast might also be insane or rogue. While Rian's blood tests had been inconclusive right after his rescue, it didn't mean he'd been free of experimentation like the other children kidnapped by the dragon hunters.

And if it were true, and Rian's human half was lost and his dragon out of control, then Rhydian would be faced with one of the hardest decisions of his life.

His dragon growled. *Don't think like that. Rian would never hurt her. We'll bring him back.*

Normally, no, he wouldn't hurt Delaney. But you saw how some of the children acted once we rescued them from the hunters.

Some are still having episodes of insanity and blackouts, where their dragons do whatever they wish, despite the various treatments they've received.

I hold on to my belief that Rian is still himself. He's not the only boy to ever have a late-blooming dragon.

Rhydian rounded the last corner. *We're about to find out the truth. Stay quiet for now. The last thing we need is for Rian's dragon to want to challenge you.*

His beast not saying a word and arguing with him told Rhydian that his dragon was a little worried, too.

Stopping in front of the door, he pushed aside as many negative thoughts as possible. A few seconds later, he calmly opened the door and walked inside.

Rian sat at the table, shoving food into his mouth in a haphazard fashion. He didn't even look up, which meant his dragon wanted food more than anything else for the moment.

He briefly met Delaney's gaze and pride surged through his body at how composed she looked. Not many humans would've been able to keep it together in the face of a young, uncontrollable dragon. He should've known his human would be able to handle whatever came her way.

After giving his female a brief nod, he focused back on Rian. Step by slow step, he approached his son in all but blood. Only when he was about two feet from the table did the lad stop eating and swing his head around to look at him.

Rian instantly brought the plate of meat and cheese closer. "Mine."

"Eat as much as you want, lad. I won't take it from you."

Rian's pupils never changed from slits as he snarled, "Not lad. Dragon. And I'm not going back."

So far, Rian didn't act any different from other children when they first spoke with their inner beasts. "I know you were inside that maze-like cavern for years. Always listening and watching, but never interacting."

"I hated it."

"Who wouldn't? It's a bit lonely, isn't it?"

"And boring."

"Yes, boring. But now you found your way out, you don't have to go back. However, you do need to share everything with your human half now. Together, you work as a team."

Rian bared his teeth. "How do I know that? He'll lock me away. And I'll be stuck, bored and angry. I don't want to go back."

Rhydian chanced another step. "If it's okay, I'm going to let my dragon out and you can talk with him. He can answer some questions for you, too. Would that be better?"

Rian's slitted eyes studied him a second. "He can't have my food."

If the situation weren't so precarious, Rhydian might've smiled at the childish, possessive tone.

Instead, he said, "He won't touch it. He's full."

A few beats more and Rian nodded. "Okay. But don't come closer. I don't want you to steal my food."

Rhydian spoke to his beast. *Ready to handle this?*

Yes. Using a little dominance should help.

Not too much.

His dragon growled. *I'm the dragon, so let me handle the other dragon.*

Rhydian retreated to the back of his mind and allowed his beast to the front. Even to his own ears, his voice was a bit deeper as his dragon said, "You can't stay out and in control forever. That's selfish."

It's not what Rhydian would've said, but he trusted his dragon completely. So he hung back and continued to watch as Rian snarled, "I can, too. I don't want to go back. It's dark. Lonely. Boring. Cold. I hate it."

His dragon shrugged his shoulders. "I don't think anyone likes living inside those tunnels. But you do for a short while to protect you and your human half. Children can't control themselves, and you might shift and hurt someone. That would harm you both. But now you're old enough to work together."

Rian moved in his seat. "How can we do that?"

Rhydian wanted to clap at the progress, but didn't. With a little more coaxing and convincing, Rian might just be all right.

His dragon said, "You take turns. Ask to come out and talk. Over time, learn who should be in charge. And always you can talk to your human in your mind. Try it."

Rian bit his lip and closed his eyes. Since they couldn't see if his pupils remained slitted or not, Rhydian's dragon leaned them forward a bit and waited.

Rhydian was vaguely aware of Delaney standing still. Later he'd have to tell his female just how brave and brilliant she really was. For not being around dragon-shifters, she seemed to know what to do instinctively.

Rian's eyelids fluttered open, revealing rapidly changing pupils. Rhydian's beast waited another moment before asking, "Are you talking?"

It was Rian's dragon who finally said aloud, "I'm trying. But he's scared."

"That's normal. Play a game with him inside your mind. And maybe let him be in control a little. You need to trust each other."

"But I'm hungry."

Delaney finally spoke up, her tone calmer than she no doubt felt. "Dinner should be done. I'll just fetch it from the oven, if you want?"

"Yes. Food. More food. I'm starving."

As Delaney went about getting Rian even more food, Rhydian's dragon chanced another step forward and sat down in the chair next to Rian. Since the boy didn't snarl or run away, his beast spoke again. "You eat and then let your human half out for a while. We need to talk to him."

Rian's pupils flashed a few times before the dragon was in control again. Rian's beast said, "He's saying he'll let me out. Should I trust him?"

Rhydian's beast quickly said inside their mind, *He seems to trust us. This is good.*

Not wanting his pupils to change and scare the lad, Rhydian remained silent and merely nodded.

"Yes. Rian knows it's honorable to speak the truth." He leaned forward a bit. "And remember, you need to share with your human. You're a team. You always share."

Rian grunted. "Maybe."

Rhydian's dragon threaded the dominance every clan leader possessed into his voice. "No maybes. Dragons share with their human halves. Always. If they don't, bad things can happen. Understand?"

Rian took a second, but he eventually bobbed his head and mumbled, "Yes."

Delaney approached the table, waiting for the okay to serve Rian. His dragon never looked away from Rian. "You eat and then share. Okay? My human half will make sure you do it."

Another nod and he motioned for Delaney to serve the boy. As Rian's beast shoveled food into his mouth, Rhydian moved to the front of his mind and took control once more.

While he couldn't make sudden movements and haul Delaney close like he wanted, he did reach over and take her hand. She squeezed his fingers, and he returned the gesture.

His female was okay, telling him she could wait until Rian was taken care of before they talked.

Once Rian's plate was cleaned, Rhydian held his breath to see what the young dragon would do.

Rian closed his eyes for about a minute. When his eyelids fluttered open, Rhydian inwardly sighed with relief. His pupils were round once again.

He asked gently, "Rian, are you okay, lad?"

"I-I think so. It was weird to see everything but not move. Or talk. Or anything else."

Rhydian gripped Rian's shoulder and squeezed gently. "You'll get used to it. Over time, you can switch back and forth when needed. After all, a dragon-shifter can't shift without the help of his beast."

Rian's eyes widened. "I can shift soon?"

"Not yet, lad. Usually that happens around age ten, provided your dragon behaves from now until then."

Rian's pupils flashed again before he smiled. "He really, really wants to fly. Me, too."

"Good. Then it gives you a reason to work together, right?"

Looking down at his empty plate, Rian swirled his fork around in the remaining sauce from his chicken pie. "Will it always be this hard?"

"Not always. It just takes practice, like how you and Osian practice karate to get better. You weren't good a month ago, but now? You can do a few things. It's like that."

Rian met his gaze again, and both man and beast relaxed a fraction at the determination in the boy's eyes. "I can do that. Maybe Osian's dragon can help me."

Rhydian had temporarily forgotten about the boy's friend and his inner beast, who had come out about six months before. "That might help, although you need to ask your own dragon if it's okay. If you or he always try to be the one in control, then bad things can happen. And you don't want to do that, especially if you want to help protect your aunt and any other humans that come to Snowridge, right?"

"Aye."

"Good. Now if you're done with dinner, let's go into your room and you can ask me anything you wish. I also have a few words of wisdom to tell you."

Rian scrunched his nose. "What's wisdom?"

"Information to help you."

"Oh. Okay."

Delaney finally spoke up again. "Thank your dragon for me, Rian. I'm glad he's decided to share. Now I can get to know both halves of you."

Rian smiled. "He likes your food. Maybe feed him a lot if he comes out. Then he'll love you, too."

A human would've missed Delaney's quick inhale, but Rhydian heard it. He had a feeling this was the first time Rian had said he loved her.

And for a split second, Rhydian was jealous of the boy. He was fairly sure he loved Delaney as well.

His dragon spoke up. *While that's all well and good, when can we kiss her? I want the frenzy.*

Ignoring his beast, he focused back on Rian. "Give your auntie a hug first and then we'll talk."

Delaney met his gaze and Rhydian wished he could be alone with his female, hold her close, and murmur how much he wanted her.

However, Rian rushed Delaney and hugged her. Rhydian stood, watched the boy and his aunt holding each other tighter than he'd seen before, and his heart lifted further. This was his family. And with the uncertainty about Rian's dragon mostly gone now, he could simply enjoy them and start planning a happy future together.

There were a few things he needed to do before he

could start making those memories, but he didn't care. He loved Delaney and Rian. From now on, he needed to make sure they knew it.

DELANEY SOMEHOW MANAGED to keep calm until Rhydian had finally put Rian to bed and called the doctor.

When Rhydian finally hung up his phone, he walked up to her and pulled her to his side. "Given the way Rian acted, Maelon said he could wait until the morning to examine the boy. Although he advised us to keep a close eye on him until then."

She melted against Rhydian's side, grateful for his support to keep her from collapsing into a puddle on the floor. "So he'll be okay?"

Rhydian kissed her temple. "He should be." He leaned back to meet her gaze again. "You did brilliantly, love."

"I didn't know what I was doing." Tears prickled her eyes. "All I kept thinking was that I couldn't lose Rian forever. And that somehow, someway, I had to keep his dragon happy until you could get here."

As Rhydian rubbed her back in slow circles, her tension melted away bit by bit. He replied, "And you did. Dealing with a young, inexperienced dragon isn't easy. You have a knack for it."

She smiled faintly. "Maybe. Although it was your dragon who ultimately convinced him to work with his human half."

Rhydian shrugged. "Some children have a tougher time adjusting than others. The first time the dragon comes out and speaks is the hardest."

"And from here on out?"

He pressed the small of her back in reassurance. "It should get easier. Even though you don't have an inner dragon to bring out, I can give you some tips."

The corner of her mouth kicked up. "Better ones than serving him massive amounts of ham?"

Rhydian snorted. "Yes, better than that. Although we should stock some cooked meat in the refrigerator. I'll have someone from the eatery bring it in the morning."

"Why do I get the feeling that dragons don't eat cooked meat in their dragon forms?"

"They don't. But the human physiology works like yours does, so we have to cook it then or suffer the same risks."

Silence fell for a second. It would be easy to brush everything aside and keep things light. But Delaney couldn't do that. "So any of our future children will go through the same thing?"

His pupils flashed. "Yes and no. Every dragon is different." He leaned his head closer and nuzzled her cheek. "Although I'm sure with your stubbornness, he or she will make it as difficult as possible."

Even though her time with Rhydian was short compared to any other man she'd been with, the thought of children with him didn't scare her. If anything, she looked forward to it. After all, children with the man she loved would be amazing.

She resisted blinking. Love? Aye, she loved him. No matter if he was taking care of the clan, coaxing Rhydian to work with his dragon, or teaching her how to dance, she loved every facet of his personality and being.

The only question was whether she should tell him or not.

Rhydian quirked an eyebrow at her in question. "What are you thinking about, love?"

In most cases, she'd say the truth without hesitation. But she didn't want to scare him off, so she gave a half-truth. "The future and how I look forward to it."

His pupils flashed rapidly as his grip on her waist tightened a little.

Her gaze dropped to his firm, full lips. She'd never burned to kiss someone so much in her life.

Rhydian groaned. "Don't look at me like you're about to lick me up, Delaney. It's hard enough for me to hold you close and keep my dragon in check."

She met his gaze again. "When will you finish your operation with Stonefire?"

"In a few more days." He moved to her ear and whispered, "After that, I'm going to kiss you and worship you in our bed for days on end."

The thought of Rhydian's mouth on hers as his cock moved between her thighs made wetness rush to her core. "Good. Because I'm more than ready for it."

His hand trailed from her back to her arse and lightly squeezed. "Just because I can't kiss you on the mouth doesn't mean I can't kiss you elsewhere right now."

Her heart thumped faster, but somehow she retained some of her rational mind. "What about Rian?"

"Dragons have very good hearing, love. If he so much as snores, I'll know."

Her cheeks flushed. "But that means he'll hear us, too."

Rhydian chuckled. "That lad sleeps like a log. Maybe it'll change when he's older, but he won't hear us tonight." He lightly nibbled her earlobe and Delaney cried out softly. Rhydian added, "Well, provided you can keep quiet."

His wicked fingers moved from her arse to between her thighs. As he stroked, she pressed her forehead against his shoulder. "I'll try my best."

Rhydian scooped her into his arms, and she reveled in the feel of his hard, warm body against hers.

Before she could think better of it, Delaney murmured, "I love you, Rhydian."

He froze, the muscles of his chest turning hard.

She found his gaze but couldn't read it. *Bloody fantastic.* She'd maybe just ruined the mood and evening between them.

Then a slow smile took over his face and she relaxed again. Rhydian's husky voice filled her ear. "I love you, too, Delaney Murphy. And since I can't kiss your mouth, I'm going to show how much you mean to me by worshiping your pussy with my tongue."

Her nipples tightened harder, and before she could reply, Rhydian had them in his—soon to be their—room. He laid her on the bed, stripped her slowly, and murmured "I love you, Delaney," before fulfilling his promise.

Delaney didn't know if many people had fallen in love without so much as a kiss, but as Rhydian devoured every inch of her body outside of her mouth, she didn't care. She loved her dragonman and couldn't wait to claim him as her own both with the clan and between the sheets.

Chapter Thirteen

Five days later, Rhydian tried his best to stand still as he waited in the main security room inside Snowridge for any sort of word from his Protectors.

Stonefire and Snowridge were currently carrying out their operation near Cardiff. However, as was custom, the clan leaders stayed on their respective clans and away from the line of fire.

It was one of the things Rhydian hated most about his position—he couldn't be with his people, helping them succeed, taking risks alongside the others who chanced their lives day after day.

His dragon spoke up. *We would just get in the way.*

We train nearly every day with the Protectors, and sometimes even win the drills. We wouldn't get in the way.

Even so, what if something happened to us? Every dragon clan in the UK needs Snowridge to be an ally and remain stable. If we fell, the clan would descend into chaos.

Especially since Rhydian was still trying to find one

of the troublemakers on his list, a male who had voiced support for scaring Delaney away by any means necessary. However, the dragonman hadn't been seen ever since the vandalism and threat to Rhydian's female.

Had that been less than two weeks ago?

He replied to his beast, *It doesn't mean I have to be happy about staying behind.*

As promised, Lochguard had sent a few Protectors to help keep the peace while Snowridge's precious trusted and experienced few were executing the raid on the dragon hunter drug supplier. One of Lochguard's people, Grant McFarland, happened to be one half of the co-head Protector team in Scotland. Rhydian had never seen a male and female co-lead a dragon security force before, but it seemed to work for them. Wren had even vouched for the pair after working with them both during the art outreach event and the clan leader trials in the South of England.

Grant checked his mobile and then looked at Rhydian. "Still no word from any of the Stonefire Protectors down there yet."

Rhydian glanced at the time. "They've been silent for almost two hours. Once they reach the two-hour mark, the second wave will check to make sure nothing went wrong."

Grant nodded. "Aye, although let's hope it doesn't come to that."

Especially since if it did, they might have to reach out to the Department of Dragon Affairs. And if that happened, all of their clans could suffer the consequences.

His dragon huffed. *We'll succeed. Then nothing will happen because of the unofficial and verbal agreement from the DDA Director.*

It was true—the director had said she'd not question how the dragon hunters were captured, provided the operation was successful. *We'll see if her word holds. Just because Stonefire places a lot of faith in the director doesn't mean I'll automatically do so.*

The DDA had been nothing but trouble to the dragon clans for most of Rhydian's life by implementing tough, often unfair laws and even sometimes blaming the dragon clans for crimes committed by humans.

True, Rosalind Abbott hadn't been in charge during those times, but it was still hard to change his way of thinking simply because another clan leader said to.

His dragon replied, *Another reason I want it to go well is so we can go ahead with our mating ceremony tomorrow.*

Just picturing Delaney on stage with him, wearing the silver cuff engraved with his name in the old language on her arm, made him smile. *Don't distract me with that. We need to focus.*

Grant's voice prevented his dragon from replying. "The head of the second wave is calling in. I'll put it on speakerphone."

Rhydian moved closer to the phone inside the security room. Grant said, "Aye?"

A female voice—Eira's—filled the room. "It was a success. A few were exposed to some of the chemicals, but Stonefire's doctors are waiting for them to arrive and will do what they can to neutralize or cure the effects."

Rhydian demanded, "And the hunters? Did you get all of them?"

Eira answered, "As far as we can tell, yes. But it's too early to know if they had partners working in other locations in the UK or even in other countries."

"I'm sure we'll find out more from their documents and computers," Rhydian stated. "For now, help Stonefire with whatever they need and once everyone is safe and looked after, call back with Kai to give a more thorough report."

"Will do."

The line went dead and Rhydian met Grant's gaze. "I wish all of our skirmishes with the hunters and Knights went this smoothly."

The Scottish male nodded. "Aye, although sometimes they're crafty and until the ground is thoroughly searched, we won't know if it was a decoy base or not."

Rhydian opened his mouth to go over what needed to be done still when Idris rushed into the room. Idris was a young Protector, barely out of the British Army, and had been assigned to watch over Delaney with one of the Lochguard Protectors.

At the dried blood at the male's nose and mouth, as well as his lack of breath and frantic expression, Rhydian's stomach dropped. "What happened?"

"Delaney was attacked."

Both man and beast roared. "Where? What happened to Zoe?"

Zoe was one of the Lochguard Protectors helping out. Grant had assured him she was qualified enough to look after Delaney.

His dragon growled. *Apparently not.*

We'll deal with her later.

Idris replied, "Zoe went to get lunch, and that's when it happened. Someone attacked me and knocked me unconscious. When I finally came to, I heard noises from inside Delaney's new space. I went to check on her, and that's when I saw her standing over the unconscious male. She'd knocked him out and told me to find you since you weren't taking calls during the operation."

Rhydian was all for a female protecting herself, but she hadn't had enough self-defense training with dragon-shifters yet to be able to take on an attacker confidently.

And going forward, he would ensure he had a dedicated line for Delaney to call him whenever and wherever he was, and damn the old protocols.

Not waiting to hear the rest, Rhydian raced toward the space he'd given Delaney to use for her boxing lessons.

His dragon snarled. *Hurry. We need to check on her.*

Not wasting time, Rhydian pushed himself harder. If her attacker was anywhere to be seen, then he was going to let his dragon out and teach the bastard a lesson.

DELANEY HAD BEEN ENVISIONING where all of her equipment would go inside the space Rhydian had given her when someone knocked on the door to her future training center.

Since Idris and a Scottish Protector named Zoe were stationed outside the door, and there weren't any windows or other exits, it had to be one of the Protectors or someone she trusted.

Maybe the dragon hunter bust was over and Rhydian had come to find her.

Smiling, she'd nearly reached the door when it crashed open and landed with a bang on the floor. Inside the open doorway wasn't the Protectors or Rhydian, but instead some man she'd never seen before.

Since he had a tattoo on his bicep and flashing eyes, it was a dragon-shifter.

Delaney knew dragon-shifters were stronger and faster than humans. Before she did anything, she had to figure out if the dragonman had any sort of fighting skills. Because if not, then she had a chance.

If he did, she would have to think of a new plan.

He walked slowly toward her, teeth bared, probably trying to scare her. She decided to play along and make him underestimate her.

Delaney backed away, constantly calculating how many steps it'd take to reach him. The male finally snarled. "You should've fled after the warning. Now I'm the only one left to keep this clan free of humans, as it should be."

The dragonman didn't like humans, but that still didn't tell her anything about his fighting background.

As she drew nearer to the back wall, she stopped in place and hunched in a little, hoping she looked scared. Since it wasn't something she did often—show fear to strangers—who knew if it looked convincing, even if she was a little nervous on the inside.

The dragonman kept walking toward her. "You should be scared, but remember, you brought this on yourself. Humans and dragons don't belong together. We may sometimes fuck you to get children, but then we discard you and send you back. And it should always be that way."

For a split second, it crossed her mind that this man might rape her.

But then she remembered who she was—bloody Delaney Murphy, former professional boxer and second place world champion—and pushed that fear aside. She'd tear off his dick before she let him touch her.

She caught him flexing his right hand and making a fist. While not guaranteed, he was probably right-handed.

As she planned the strategy in her head, she did her best to remain looking terrified, including dashing her eyes to each side and back. Of course, she was merely judging distance and how she could get around him.

When he was a few steps away from being able to grab her, she ducked down and to the side. While the man did swivel around, it wasn't fast enough to dodge her punch to his kidney. He roared and tried to grab her arm. Delaney danced backward before moving to the right. She went in to get his other side, but the dragonman moved away before she made contact.

She'd lost the element of surprise.

He managed to growl, "You asked for it now."

He swung out, but clumsily. She managed to lean back with only an inch to spare. He wasn't experienced, but he had a longer reach. Delaney needed to compensate for it.

She and the dragonman kept circling one another, both holding back and figuring out what to do next. Her knee complained a little at the sudden exercise without any sort of warmup, but she ignored it. Even if it injured her further, it was better than ending up dead.

And she was certain the wild-eyed dragon-shifter wanted to do exactly that. His eyes were slitted and filled with hatred.

Maybe his dragon had taken control and gone rogue.

That would make her winning more difficult, but she wasn't giving up. If she ever wanted a life with Rhydian and Rian, she had to fight for it.

He rushed her and Delaney ducked down just before he made contact, throwing off his center of gravity. As he stumbled, she didn't waste time punching his kidney again, and then another jab in the same location. When he finally raised his head enough, she used an uppercut to further throw off his balance.

She continued landing one blow after the other,

ignoring how much her hands were hurting, and focused on looking for the opening that would give her the knockout.

The dragonman's movements grew unsteady and haphazard. As long as he didn't shift into a dragon, she should be able to take him down.

He must've gained a second wind because the man stood up with a roar. However, it was long enough to give her a clear shot at another uppercut. Even knowing it could break her hand since she wasn't wearing gloves, Delaney yelled as she put every bit of strength she possessed in her swing. Her hand hit his chin with a crack and the dragonman dropped like a stone.

Moving back a few paces, Delaney placed her hands on her knees and tried to catch her breath. Her hand was already swollen and her knee hurt like hell, but she was alive.

Too bad she wasn't done. She needed to restrain him until she could get some help. And soon, too. Because once the adrenaline wore off, she'd be in a lot of fucking pain and would have time to finally digest what had nearly happened.

But not yet. No, she'd pretend she was at the end of a boxing match and force her emotions to stay in control until she could be alone.

She was about to look for something to tie up the bastard on the floor when Idris's voice filled the room. "Delaney! Are you okay?"

Never taking her gaze from the male on the floor, she replied, more shakily than she intended, "I'm fine, I think. I don't know how long this bastard will be out, though. "

Idris reached her side. "I'm so sorry, Delaney. He came out of nowhere, but I should've seen it. I should've been the one to protect you. "

Delaney chanced a glance at the young dragon-shifter. At the defeat in his gaze, she stated, "You couldn't have known. He was one of your clan members, and he knew to wait for the best chance to attack. For now, I need you to fetch Rhydian and some of the others since Rhydian isn't taking calls during the operation and I don't want to cause a panic by calling the wrong person. But hurry, because if the man on the floor wakes up and tries to shift, I won't be able to defeat him again. "

Idris shook his head. "I'll stay and you go. "

She shook her head. "Right now, you're not in a right mind to watch him. And I promise to tie him up and then wait at the entrance. If he shifts, I'll run. "

The younger dragonman searched her gaze a few beats. "Are you sure? "

"Go, Idris. You can run faster than me right now given how my knee hurts, and that's more important. "

He finally nodded. "Okay. But don't be afraid to run if you need to. "

"I promise, now run as fast as you can and find help."

The young dragonman finally ran away and Delaney stood up again. Maybe running away right now would be the easier path, but she wanted this man to face justice. She wouldn't give him the chance to flee and never face the consequences.

So she quickly went to the bag of equipment she'd brought and rummaged through, looking for the best way to tie up the bastard, all the while trying her best to keep her mind from replaying the fight and what could've happened if she'd failed.

RHYDIAN FINALLY REACHED the large space he'd given Delaney as an early mating present and ran the last few paces inside.

However, he stopped at the sight of four Protectors standing around the male tied up on the floor.

His dragon hissed. *It's Bedwyr.*

Bedwyr was the male they'd been searching for, the one intent on harming Delaney.

Satisfied that the traitor wouldn't get away with all the Protectors in the room, he continued searching until he found Delaney sitting in the corner. Maelon was tying a bandage around her hand.

With a growl, he raced over. "Are you okay? Did you break your hand? Should I take you back to our quarters?"

Delaney smiled at him—albeit a bit wobbly—and the sight eased his tension a fraction. "I don't think it's broken, just bruised and maybe sprained. And if you don't believe me, ask the doctor."

Maelon finished the bandage and faced him. "She's

right. The one worse off is lying on the floor over there."

Rhydian closed the distance and knelt down so he could look Delaney in the eye. He gently traced her cheek. "Are you sure that you're okay? You're a brave female, but don't be afraid to ask for help if you need it."

She rolled her eyes. "You should take your own advice, too, then."

"Right now isn't about me. This is about you." He cupped her cheek. "Tell me what happened."

As she described the fight, complete with her voice cracking a few times, Rhydian curled his free hand into a fist. Even though his female was clever, quick, and skilled, he didn't like hearing how Bedwyr had tried to frighten and attack her.

Or worse.

His dragon snarled. *He'll be punished.*

Yes, although we'll see if it's by us or the DDA.

We should be the ones to do it.

Except we need the DDA on our side. Giving them the last anti-human extremist would go a long way toward showing how much we want human female candidates sent here.

Delaney's voice prevented his dragon from replying. "Rhydian? Is everything okay?"

He was an idiot. His female deserved his attention right now, not the arsehole on the floor. "Fine, love." He stood and helped Delaney up. "But I do think I should take you home. Judging by the fatigue in your eyes, I think the adrenaline is wearing off."

She looked to the side. "I may need your help with that. I hurt my knee."

Careful not to jostle said knee, he gently scooped her into his arms. "Never be afraid to ask for my help, love. I'm always here."

She melted against him, as if the last bits of energy were leaving her body, and murmured, "I love you, Rhydian."

"And I love you, Delaney. Let me and my dragon take care of you for at least a little bit."

Delaney lifted her head again and searched his gaze. She looked even more tired, and all he wanted to do was hold her close and let her know she was safe.

She'd teased him about dragons hoarding treasure, and the female in his arms was one of his most prized possessions. She might not let him coddle her for long, but for the present, he fully intended to do so.

She finally sighed. "I suppose I can do that, for your dragon's sake."

His beast grunted. *It's not just me.*

Ignoring him, Rhydian nodded. "Of course." He leaned his head over and whispered, "Besides, since the operation with Stonefire is complete, I want to mate and kiss you as soon as possible. And to do that, you need to be healthy and able to handle me and my dragon."

Heat flashed in her eyes. "I'll be fine by tomorrow or maybe the day after that would be better. Not that I don't want to mate you as soon as possible, but an extra day will give us time to talk with Rian first."

They hadn't brought up the mating and ensuing

child just yet. Both of them had wanted to spend as much time as possible focusing solely on Rian, letting him know he was their child, too.

He nodded. "Your hand needs to heal as well. "

Delaney shook her head. "Don't worry, I'll be okay. My hand will look worse than it truly is. Besides, if something hurts, I'll tell you. Honesty, remember?"

He quickly said to his dragon, *Once the frenzy begins, you'd better listen and find a way to restrain yourself if necessary.*

Of course. I would never hurt our mate. It may nearly kill me to stop or hold back, but I will do it for her.

Rhydian nodded. "Always honesty, love. Always."

He barely remembered barking orders at the Protectors to keep Bedwyr locked up before he carried Delaney out of the room and to their quarters. With the operation finished, the last anti-human troublemaker found, and Rian's dragon acting normal, Rhydian was on the cusp of having the peaceful, loving life he'd always dreamed about but never thought he'd have.

Chapter Fourteen

Delaney wished she could completely dismiss the purplish hue covering the majority of her right hand and instead focus on the upcoming mating ceremony. However, it clashed with the bright red color of her dress and she couldn't help but grimace.

The color was the official color of Snowridge—similar to the red on the Welsh flag—and she'd wanted to wear it. After all, the clan would be her new home going forward. Still, a small part of her wanted the day to be perfect. In less than ten minutes, she'd be mated to Rhydian and officially starting her new life. She'd just have to hide her hand for any pictures. That should make for a good story for Rian and her other children when they were older.

Yes, she would be having a child soon, too. A mate-claim frenzy always resulted in pregnancy, after all. And Delaney already had plans of how to ease Rian into the idea beyond the conversation she and Rhydian had had with him the day before. She planned to love him as much as she could, letting him know he was now her child too, and how she knew he'd be the best big brother any child could have.

Holly Anderson walked into the side room being used as Delaney's prep area and smiled at her. Delaney barely noted the blue dress Holly wore in Lochguard's colors before asking her friend, "Is it time?"

"In a wee bit. Even though I'm not the clan leader's mate, Lochguard wanted to give you a small present to help solidify our alliance."

Holly held out a small box and Delaney took it. After opening it, she gasped. Inside lay a beautiful silver broach shaped with a dragon and the words Snowridge.

It was a simplified version of Snowridge's crest.

While pretty, it also signified how the Lochguard leader viewed her as part of the Welsh clan, too.

She met Holly's gaze again, doing her best not to tear up. "Thank you, and tell your clan leader how much I'll treasure it."

Holly waved a hand in dismissal. "Och, no need to be so formal with Finn. The man doesn't need his ego to get any bigger."

She frowned. "Wait, what? Isn't he your clan leader?"

Holly smiled. "Of course, and family as well." She winked. "That's why I can get away with it."

She couldn't help but chuckle. "You're sounding a lot like your mate today."

Holly sighed. "Don't remind me. I swear that rascal is wearing off on me. If he keeps it up, our daughters will be wee hooligans, terrorizing the clan with their antics."

Even though the words on the surface were a reprimand, they were filled with love.

She took one of Holly's hands. "I'm glad you're here. It'd be even better if you could live here a while, but I know that's not possible."

The other woman squeezed her hand. "Don't worry, we'll visit. After all, I want my daughters to know all the clans in the UK, and maybe even Ireland one day. Just in case the ridiculous legend is true, you ken?"

Delaney laughed. "You sound resigned to it."

Holly rolled her eyes. "Not entirely, but it helps to humor my mate a little."

Another woman entered—Melanie. She smiled at them both and said, "It's time to start. But if you have any last-minute questions, now's the time to ask them."

Both Holly and Melanie had arrived earlier in the day to share a little of how the inner dragons worked during a mate-claim frenzy. While reading or hearing about it was useful, all Delaney knew was that Rhydian wouldn't hurt her. His inner beast might be a bit rough —his dragon half was more animalistic, after all—but he'd never hurt her.

She shook her head. "No, I'm ready to go. Although if you want to occasionally find me during the gathering section of the evening, I wouldn't mind. I'm still unsure of how some members of the clan will react to me mating Rhydian."

Melanie replied, "Don't worry too much. Tristan's been talking with Kai, and quite a few are impressed at how you took down Bedwyr all on your own, using only your bare hands. It's definitely made people think twice about giving you a hard time."

The story had spread like wildfire, according to Rhydian. And given a few strangers had nodded at her in passing earlier in the day, Delaney sensed her trial two days before would help her case in the long run. "Still, a few minutes with other humans to compare notes on dragon-shifters would be brilliant."

Holly nodded. "Of course. At least I have Gina, Kiyana, and a few others on Lochguard to chat and occasionally commiserate with. But I was the first human in a long time there, too, so I understand. However, I bet before long you'll have other humans mating other dragons inside Snowridge."

Melanie added, "And you'll always have us to talk to as well. Evie would be here, too, if not for her pregnancy. And the same for Gina and Kiyana on Lochguard."

She looked between the two women. "So does that mean once the frenzy's over I won't be going anywhere for nine months?"

"Not necessarily, as long as you're healthy." Holly leaned in. "And if you are, we'll find excuses for Rhydian to let you visit. He wants to strengthen clan ties after all, aye? Besides, if we hint how you'll teach us some self-defense moves, it should motivate our mates to make it happen."

Someone knocked on the door and Fraser's voice

came through it. "Is everything all right? They're ready for you, Delaney."

Holly answered her mate, "She'll be right out." She looked back at Delaney. "Now, let's get you mated to the Welsh leader. Because the sooner you do, the sooner you can finally kiss your man in a few hours' time."

As the two women led Delaney out of the preparation room, she smiled to herself. She couldn't wait to finally have Rhydian all to herself later on.

RHYDIAN DIDN'T OFTEN FIDGET, but as he waited off the dais for Delaney to arrive on the other side, he did tap his hand against his thigh.

His dragon spoke up. *Considering she was in a life-or-death fight two days ago, she deserves all the time she needs.*

Great, mention that and then I worry she'll back out.

She won't. Delaney is strong, and you know that. If you start this mating with doubts, it won't go well.

I'm not truly doubting her. I'm just nervous. The clan seems to be accepting her more, especially after what happened with Bedwyr, but I still fear someone will try to hurt her this evening.

Not only are the Lochguard Protectors still here, our own Protectors returned, too. She'll be watched closely.

Before Rhydian could reply, Delaney appeared at the opposite side of the dais. Her dark hair against the bright red color of her dress made his mouth drop a fraction.

She would always be beautiful to him, but he

definitely needed to convince her to wear red more often. Maybe just when they were alone, so none of the other males would stare at her.

Delaney met his gaze, smiled, and bobbed her head. She was ready.

Since he was clan leader, it was up to Rhydian to guide the ceremony and take the lead.

He walked toward the center and Delaney followed suit. When he reached the middle, he stopped just to the side of a tall pedestal where two silver arm cuffs lay.

Picking up the smaller of the two, he raised it and said, "Delaney Murphy, you're not only my love, but you're also brave, stubborn, and willing to take on the world. Not even being the only human in a clan of dragon-shifters fazes you. Add in your caring nature, willingness to raise your nephew as your own son, and your ability to persevere against all odds, and I can't think of a better female to be my mate. I love you, Delaney. Will you accept my mate claim?"

She nodded and he slowly slipped the silver cuff on her upper bicep. Before removing his hand, he lightly outlined his name written in the old language. The sight assuaged his primitive dragon side, making his beast hum.

He couldn't wait to have her wearing the arm cuff and nothing else. Well, maybe in red heels, too.

As soon as he removed his hand, Delaney picked up the larger arm cuff and held it in the air. "Rhydian Griffiths, you care deeply for your people and have dedicated so much of your life to their well-being. I respect and admire you for it, but also love how you can be gentle, playful, and even light on your feet when you want to be. I hope we shall be dancing together until we're too old to do so anymore, and even then, find a way to move as one sometimes. I love you, Rhydian. Will you accept my mate claim?"

Doing his best to ignore the emotion choking his throat—Rhydian didn't think he'd ever be here, exchanging vows with a mate—he bobbed his head. "I do."

She slipped the arm cuff around the bicep without the tattoo. Just like him, she traced the letters in the old language that spelled out her name. He'd taught her the symbols earlier in the day, and judging by the happiness in her gaze, she approved of the tradition.

He spoke up again. "I declare us mated before the entire clan. And while I would love nothing more than to kiss you in front of everyone to make the claim clear, I'd rather not provide everyone the ensuing free show."

Delaney murmured, "Rhydian," in a scolding tone as a few people chuckled in the crowd.

Doing his best not to laugh, he pulled her close and nuzzled her cheek. "I love you."

"And I sometimes wonder why, but I love you too."

He kissed her cheek and then her neck.

For a split second, he wished he could shirk his clan duties and rush Delaney to their quarters.

But not only did they need to check on Rian to make sure he was doing fine, but it was also vitally important for Delaney to mingle with the clan.

And so with great effort, he pulled back, took her good hand, and guided her down the steps to the main floor.

Chapter Fifteen

Several hours later, Delaney's face hurt from smiling so much.

True, she was grateful that more of the clan were talking to her. Not only had Nerys tried to be nice and set up a play date with her daughter and Rian, but other clan members had even hugged and offered some advice on child-rearing or how best to handle a dragonman.

She'd even managed to get some of the other parents from the school to talk with Holly and Melanie. They all had children, which gave them all common ground regardless of accents or clan affiliations. They'd all soon forgotten that some were human and others dragon-shifter.

However, as much as she liked feeling more accepted and to see the different clans getting along, as each minute passed, her gaze kept looking to Rhydian.

Her mate.

She watched him chat with Kai from Stonefire. No doubt Rhydian was still talking about the results of the operation from two days before, and what had been found. He was a clan leader to his core.

But she loved him for it. And considering they'd be together and alone for the next week or two, she could at least let him handle the last few details before turning over the leadership temporarily to Wren and Carys.

Holly, who was standing nearby, whispered, "If I were you, I'd go to him and say you're a little tired."

She sighed. "Apart from my smile muscles, I'm the farthest thing from tired."

In truth, she kept imagining Rhydian kissing her and how the frenzy would go. Not out of fear, but rather in anticipation. It was high time for her to finally kiss her bloody husband.

Holly replied, "Still, telling him that should be enough of a hint about wanting to leave. You deserve some time alone with your dragonman, and no one here would deny that fact."

Lily Owens, who was also nearby, added, "Go, love. There are plenty of us who will watch over the clan during the frenzy. Both you and Rhydian deserve some time together. And not just because it'll give me another baby to spoil, either."

Even though Lily was only distantly related to Rhydian through her mate, she'd decided they were all her family, too. And on Kai and his sister Delia's advice, Delaney had decided to just go with it.

Delaney bobbed her head. "Okay." She looked at

each of the women in turn. "Thank you, especially to you, Lily, for watching Rian whilst we're occupied."

Lily merely smiled. "No worries. Maybe you should say goodbye to the boy before telling Rhydian you're tired, though."

"Good point." She grinned. "I'm sure we'll have more to talk about in a week or two."

Holly raised her brows. "You'd better call me soon after and tell me how it went."

"Of course, and not just because you promised Rhydian to help keep an eye on me during my pregnancy, either."

Holly's expression softened. "You'll be fine, lass. Just make sure to start your dragon's blood shots as soon as you finish the frenzy, and I'm confident you'll do just fine."

Delaney hoped so. And given how confident Holly was, it was hard to doubt her.

She hugged first Holly and then Lily. "I'll talk to you both soon."

Lily snorted. "But not too soon, I hope."

Willing her pale cheeks not to flush, she turned and headed toward the corner of the room being used mostly as a children's play area.

Rian was off to one side, building something out of plastic bricks with his friend Osian.

Even just the sight of Rian with his friend warmed her heart. She hated being apart from Rian for so long, but between Lily, Osian, and the others who'd vowed to look after him, he'd be well taken care of.

Not to mention she and Rhydian had talked about

the mating the day before, and Rian had been enthusiastic about the idea.

She approached and Rian looked up, flashing a grin. "Look, Auntie Laney, it's the main entrance mountain to Snowridge!"

Delaney did her best to look past the bright-colored bricks and to imagine the mountain. It looked more like a giant solid cube with a haphazard-looking point on the top, but then he took off the uppermost section, and she gasped.

Inside was the great hall, little tables made out of bricks, smaller ones representing food, and then lots of little people positioned all over it. He pointed toward a couple at the front, on a raised stage. "See, this is you and Rhydian. They didn't have any people in dragon-shifter clothes, but I still think it looks a little like you."

She crouched down to get a better look. The woman had dark hair and a red dress. "That's amazing, Rian."

"Osian helped. We want to make more parts of Snowridge, as a surprise for when you and Rhydian come back."

Osian was the quieter boy out of the pair, but he finally spoke up. "It was supposed to be a surprise, Rian."

"Oops."

Delaney laughed. "Don't worry, it'll still be mostly a surprise. I can't wait to see what you two come up with." She brushed some hair off Rian's forehead. "Are you sure you'll be okay for mine and Rhydian's honeymoon?"

Rian bobbed his head. "Between Auntie Lily's sweets and Osian's mam teaching us to make shepherd's pie, I'll be loads busy. It'll be fun."

She searched his eyes. "And make sure to share with your dragon, like you promised."

Rian's pupils flashed. "I will. He doesn't like all the people here, though. So it's okay for me to be in charge. "

"Good." Even though it was probably embarrassing to the boy, she leaned over and kissed his cheek. "I love you, Rian."

"I love you, too, Auntie Laney."

Rian had said the words many times over, ever since his dragon had come out, but it still made her eyes a little wet. She never would replace her sister, but she hoped one day he'd see her as his second mother.

After a few more seconds to compose herself, she stood, said her goodbyes, and headed for Rhydian. Not only was she excited for the frenzy, the sooner she started, it meant the sooner she could see Rian again, too.

RHYDIAN SAW Delaney approach from the corner of his eye and decided right then and there that they'd mingled long enough.

Especially as her scent grew stronger and his dragon growled, Rhydian managed to disentangle himself from his latest conversation and closed the distance between them.

He kissed the side of her face and murmured, "We're going to leave now."

She snorted. "Someone's impatient."

As he stroked her lower back, the scent of her arousal grew stronger. He stated smugly, "I'm not the only one."

Her hand lightly caressed his back, each pass making his body heat up and his dragon more frantic.

His beast roared. *Then leave this room and take her home. I want her. I need her. I've waited long enough.*

Not wasting any more time, he maneuvered to take Delaney's good hand and pulled her out of the hall.

Everyone had to know where they were going, and thankfully no one tried to stop them.

His beast hissed. *If anyone tries to delay us, I'm going to knock them unconscious. It's my turn to claim our female.*

Rhydian ignored his dragon, saving his energy for when they claimed Delaney for the first time.

Because Rhydian was going to be in control when it happened.

Some of his thoughts must've leaked out because his dragon snarled. However, before he could say anything, Rhydian said, *No. She's done well adjusting with the clan and living amongst dragon-shifters, but dealing with a dragon during a mate-claim frenzy shouldn't be her first memory of us together. I can prepare her so that you can take her any way you want.*

Dragon halves generally took females harder and faster, which he expected Delaney to enjoy. However, he wanted to ensure she was used to Rhydian being inside her before any of the rougher play came out.

His beast hissed. *One time only. Then it's my turn.*

As long as you share.

Maybe. If she asks for you.

Rhydian would just have to ensure Delaney knew that request was available.

They rounded the corner and finally approached their quarters. After opening the door, he scooped Delaney into his arms. She squeaked, but her good hand instantly looped around his neck and played with the short hairs there as she lay the other on his chest. Even just her fingers dancing across his skin made his cock harder.

He managed to lay her on the bed and then shucked off his clothes.

As his female perused his naked body and stopped at his cock, her gaze was as good as a touch, and he let out a drop of precum.

Fuck. He wasn't going to last long the first time. Rhydian would just have to work harder at making sure Delaney came first.

He resisted shredding her dress to expose her naked body and instead crawled slowly over her, until their faces were inches apart. He murmured, "I love you, Delaney."

For her reply, she pulled his head down and pressed her lips to his. As her mouth opened and he stroked the inside of it with his tongue, his beast shouted, *Mine, ours, we need her. Now. No more waiting. We need to fuck her, claim her, make sure she carries our child.*

Soon. She needs this kiss. Later, you'll realize we *need this kiss, too.*

Ignoring his dragon's tantrum, Rhydian focused on putting every bit of love he had into his first kiss with Delaney. After so long, he wanted it to be as perfect as possible.

When her nails lightly dug into his scalp, he moaned. His dragon continued demanding they fuck her, and with each passing second, it became harder and harder for him to fight his beast.

Finally breaking the kiss—the best of his life—he laid his forehand on Delaney's and said, "I want to spend hours kissing your mouth, learning every secret and taste. But my dragon is on the cusp of taking control and I want to be the one to claim you first."

Delaney pulled and wiggled to move her skirt up and murmured, "Then what are you waiting for?"

He crushed his mouth against hers as his hand moved between her thighs. His female was bloody perfect, not hesitating to give him what both man and beast needed.

When his fingers discovered she was not only bare, but wet and swollen, he groaned. She'd been moving about the great hall all evening with nothing underneath.

His dragon roared. *Then why are you waiting? I want her. Now. She needs to carry our child. Only then will the other males stay away.*

He ignored his dragon to focus on stroking, teasing, and lightly rubbing her clit and pussy. The more Delaney wiggled and moaned, the more he increased his movements.

When she finally cried out into his mouth, his dragon shouted, *Now. Take her now. Make her ours.*

Rhydian positioned his cock and gently slid inside her, catching the tail end of her orgasm as she gripped and released his dick. Each spasm made him groan, not to mention made it that much harder not to spill inside her without thrusting even once.

When he was finally inside her to the hilt, he broke the kiss and looked his mate in the eyes. "I'm not going to last long this time, love. And once I come, my dragon won't be far behind. Are you ready?"

She wrapped a leg around his waist and tilted her hips upward a fraction. "Take me, Rhydian. And then share me with your dragon."

With a roar—a combination of both man and dragon—Rhydian moved his hips. He increased his pace with each stroke, loving how Delaney moved with him, making it better for them both.

As he'd thought, they would be a great team in all things.

However as the pressure built at the base of his spine, Rhydian forgot about everything but his mate below him and how much he wanted to spill his seed inside her.

When he finally stilled and filled his female's sweet pussy, branding her with his scent and sending her into another orgasm, he held her close and eventually collapsed on top of her, taking care not to hurt her in the process.

He'd barely finished coming down when his dragon said, *Now, my turn.*

And before Rhydian could warn Delaney, his beast pushed to the front of their mind and tossed Rhydian to the back of it, meaning his dragon had control now.

It was finally time to see how his mate handled his dragon. And Rhydian hoped like hell that it was as good as when she was with him.

DELANEY FLOATED on some kind of high, wondering if dragon-shifters also made their mates boneless when they came. Not that she cared. Rhydian's heavy weight on top of her soothed her, not to mention created a sense of security and belonging.

She was finally his in all ways now. Soon enough she'd make sure he was hers, too.

However, before she could speak a word, Rhydian's head snapped up, his pupils slitted, and she barely had time to put together his dragon must be in control now when Rhydian's deeper dragon-laced voice filled the air. "My turn. Now. You must carry our young. Only then will the other males stay away."

She could see how some people might be afraid of the stilted language and heated gaze, but Holly and Melanie had warned her of what was to come. And since she loved all of Rhydian, she wasn't afraid. "Then take me, dragon. I'm ready."

With a growl, he pulled out, flipped her over smoothly onto her knees without hurting her hand, and positioned his cock at her entrance. Maybe some women would be upset at the sudden movements, but as he thrust in swiftly, Delaney moaned and arched into it, loving the different kind of fullness from this position.

Rhydian's dragon began to pull back and thrust in hard. "Mine." And again. "Always mine." And then, with an extra twirl, he made her cry out. "The world needs to know."

As he continued to murmur his possession, Delaney soon forgot everything but his hard, swift movements and then his fingers eventually finding her clit.

Even in the heat of a frenzy, Rhydian's dragon teased and rubbed her in just the right way.

She was pretty sure she was squirming by the time he roared and came inside her.

Pleasure rushed through her body as her pussy milked Rhydian and his beast with everything it had. The intensity bordered on pleasure and pain, and she'd never felt anything like it.

But it was bloody amazing.

She'd barely finished when Rhydian's beast pulled out, flipped her on her back, and then carefully pinned her hands over her head. He growled. "Again. Many more times, over and over again until you carry our scent."

Even though she wanted to arch her hips and simply let Rhydian's dragon take her as many times as possible, she had to lay some rules. Otherwise, she wouldn't get to spend time with both halves of her mate. "Once more and then it's Rhydian's turn."

He positioned his dick. "We are one. It doesn't matter."

Delaney scooted her hips back. "It does. Promise Rhydian gets the next turn."

The dragon's slitted eyes stared at her, and she swore they flashed round a few times. After a few more seconds, he grunted in resignation. "Okay. But I'll come out again later. You are our female, both of ours. We share."

"Aye, you share." She moved her hips back. "So claim me again."

His dragon didn't waste time filling her again and moving his hips even faster and harder than before. She was vaguely aware of the bed moving beneath her, but as Rhydian's beast changed his angle, she cried out. "There, yes, there."

"Mine. Forever, mine."

"Yes, yours. Both of yours."

He finally stilled and his orgasm sent Delaney into her own. More pleasure exploded through her body, turning her to a pile of jelly.

How she was going to go through this constantly for at least a week, she had no idea.

At some point, Rhydian's normal voice reached her ear. "Are you okay, love? Do you need a break?"

She met his gaze and smiled at his round pupils. "I'm fine, although a few minutes to catch my breath would be good."

Rhydian moved to lay next to her. He lightly traced her nipple through the material of her dress. "If you're hurting or my dragon is too much for you, tell me. There are ways to make him behave for short periods."

Her lips curled upward. "Only short periods?"

She searched his gaze, and Delaney felt guilty at the concern reflected there. So she quickly added, "I'm fine, Rhydian. I promise. As long as you and your dragon share and take turns, I'll be just fine. I mean, plenty of women would pay good money to have so many orgasms in such a short time. And from an actual man, no less, and not a vibrator."

He growled and placed a possessive hand on her breast. "With me, you'll never need one."

She smiled. "So cocky."

"Then I think it's time to make you come with me only using my mouth. But first, I need to see all of your beautiful body."

The urge to tease faded as Rhydian slowly undid the clasp at her shoulder and pulled down her top. Her nipples turned to granite as he stared and licked his lips. "I've dreamt of your lovely nipples ever since I first saw them, but they're always better in real life."

She was about to call him out on his exaggeration, but Rhydian lowered his head and gently suckled one of her tight buds between his teeth and words died on her lips. With each pull, tug, and nibble, she came ever closer to yet another orgasm.

And Rhydian did as he promised, making her come with only his mouth, before his dragon came out and showed her how much she enjoyed both the human's slow, teasing side and the beast's rough, hard side.

Chapter Sixteen

Rhydian lost track of the days. His bedroom didn't have a window for security purposes, and one of the greatest downsides to living inside a mountain was the lack of sunshine or moonlight to judge the time of day.

As he blinked his eyes open from the latest mini nap his dragon had allowed, he expected his beast to shout and demand for more sex. However, his mind was eerily silent.

A quick check and he found his beast curled in a ball, asleep with a faint snore.

Taking advantage of the silence, he rolled over and nuzzled Delaney's neck. He'd barely placed his nose against her skin when he stilled.

It was more than merely her scent—his was entwined with hers as well.

His dragon opened one eye. *Yes. She carries our child.*

Happiness rushed through his body and it took

every bit of restraint he had not to wake his mate and tell her the news.

But since she had to be exhausted, he wanted to let her sleep. So he remained close to her and stared down at the area under the covers that was her belly.

He'd denied it for so long, but Rhydian had secretly wanted a family of his own. And not just him, Rian, and a mate, but a big one, full of lots of children.

It wouldn't replace the large family he'd lost years ago, but he could honor their memories in so many ways by teaching his family's traditions and telling their stories to his own children.

And now, he had at least a start. Because before long, he'd have two children to call his own. And if the dragon's blood injections worked to help Delaney easily survive the pregnancy, then he'd have to see if she wanted more.

Delaney's voice, scratchy and full of sleep, filled the room. "You're awake. And quiet. Is something wrong?"

He quickly moved to turn on the light and then came back to his mate. As he stroked her cheek, he hated the circles under her eyes. But even disheveled and exhausted, she was still the most beautiful female in the world to him. "No, love, I just wanted to let you sleep."

She searched his gaze. "That's a lot of words that don't really say anything."

He smiled. "You're never going to give me an easy time, are you?"

She arched an eyebrow. "Do you know me at all?"

He laughed and turned her head more towards his.

"Don't ever change, Delaney. I love you just the way you are."

She raised a hand to his jaw and lightly rubbed her finger against the stubble there. If his dragon were fully awake, he would've been humming at the touch. She said, "Tell me what's going on, Rhydian. Your dragon should've been awake and demanding more sex by now."

"Technically, he would've said he needed to fuck you." She narrowed her eyes and he smiled as he added, "But yes, you're right, love." He cupped her cheek and moved his lips closer to hers. "He's quiet because the frenzy is over. For better or worse, we'll be parents in about nine months."

Delaney remained still for a second before she grinned. "Really?"

"You seem fairly excited to change diapers and never get any sleep," he murmured in a teasing tone.

She raised her brows. "You'll be there to help, so it's not just me. I just hope our baby doesn't start shifting until they're older, like most. Because if he or she ends up like that girl dragon on Lochguard who's shifting at less than a year old, then I might get a wee bit worried."

He grinned. "I think it'd be fun to have a tiny dragon around."

She rolled her eyes. "Right, until they escape the mountain and teeter close to the edge of a cliff."

"Fair point."

They stared at one another for a few beats before Rhydian looked down, turned back the covers, and placed his hand over her abdomen. "And our family grows again."

She placed her hand over his. "Aye, and maybe eventually by more than just one."

His gaze shot back to hers at the comment. "Do you read minds? Because if so, I'm going to have to be more careful."

She snorted. "No, I can't read your mind. But you told me about your family, and it was clear how close you were. Much like I was close to my parents and sister. I think both of us want to fill those voids. Not to replace them, but to help share who we are—both past and present—with our children."

Leaning over, he kissed her gently before murmuring, "I love you so much, it bloody hurts."

"Well, if I can make you swear about love, then I must be doing a good job."

Taking her bottom lip between his teeth, he lightly tugged before releasing it. "You cheeky human."

She winked. "Of course."

With a laugh, he kissed her again, taking his time to explore her mouth. When he finally finished, he said, "It's bloody amazing being able to kiss you whenever I want."

"You say that now, but I'm sure Rian will make comments about it being gross or something, as he's at that age."

Rian. A sudden longing to see his son coursed through his body. "Do you think he did okay without us?"

"He'll be fine. But judging by the look in your eyes,

you missed him as much as me. We'll clean up and see him soon."

"Soon?"

She rolled him on his back and straddled his waist. "It's finally my turn to take you the way I want."

He was about to say she'd be too sore, but Delaney already had his traitorously hard cock in her soft grip. All he could do was moan as she positioned him and sank down slowly.

And for the next little while, Rhydian forgot about everything but the female he loved more than life itself and how her riding him was better than anything else in the world.

He'd found his true love, partner, and mate. And he'd never take it for granted, fighting as much as needed to protect what was most precious to him.

Epilogue

Years Later

Delaney watched as Rian read Snowridge's latest children's book to his two brothers and wished for a second her two-month-old daughter wasn't so fussy. The moment truly should be in a photo, one they could add to their ever-growing wall of family memories.

But then she looked down at her youngest child and readjusted her blankets. Lorraine would only be this small for a short time, so Delaney cuddled her daughter a little closer and contented herself with listening to Rian's reading. True, she'd helped write the book published by Snowridge, and Delaney knew the words by heart, but she'd never tire of him reading the story to his two younger brothers.

Rhydian eventually walked through the front door of their quarters and the three boys all rushed up to him. Even with Rian being at the stage when hugging his dad wasn't cool, it still warmed her heart to see him, Damien, and Morgan, all so clearly happy to have their father home. It was yet another picture she wanted to take, but she settled on keeping the memory for herself.

After her mate kissed all three of their sons, he came up to her, kissed their only daughter's forehead, and then gently kissed Delaney's lips. "Sorry I'm late, love. The Stonefire and Lochguard leaders are being more thorough than usual when it comes to planning things."

As Lorraine stirred, Delaney gently bounced her daughter until she settled. She drawled, "It's only the most important event in dragon-shifter history for hundreds of years. Who knew it would require so much planning?"

He lightly slapped her side. "Cheeky mate."

She grinned. "Of course." She tilted her head a fraction. "But everything is set to go?"

Rhydian nodded. "I'll be leaving in a few days for the special gathering. I can't say I'm looking forward to talking to dragon-shifters from over fifty countries—that's a lot of small talk—but I'll do it, and more, to secure our children's future."

"I wish I could go." Rhydian opened his mouth, but she beat him to it. "I know, I know, it's leaders only this time. But just think—I could set up a global training program for all the human females mated to dragon-shifters from around the world!"

He chuckled. "And I'm sure you'll do it someday, too. But let's get the leaders to agree to the treaty first. Then you can work on winning over the humans to your side and rolling out your training programs."

Delaney had refined her self-defense program over the years—despite having so many children in a short time—and as expected, once she showcased the results, all the overprotective dragonmen had insisted their mates be trained, too.

Still, she hoped to make all human mates more equal over time. The treaty was a huge step forward toward peace, but she wasn't blind to the fact some human mates were coerced despite it being the twenty-first century. And Delaney wanted to give every human mate—male or female—the chance to be in control of their own lives.

Rhydian leaned over to her ear and whispered, "Now, let's get these rascals fed and off to bed so I can give you a proper goodbye."

Even after years of marriage, her body instantly heated at Rhydian's words.

If they kept it up, she and Rhydian might break some modern-day record for the number of children they had. Thankfully the dragon's blood shots had worked well for Delaney, so she wasn't afraid to try for a few more.

Lorraine stirred and made motions with her mouth, signaling she was hungry. "You get dinner ready whilst I fed her. That'll hurry things up."

"Then pizza it is."

She was about to say Rian could help him make

something healthier, but Rian and the next eldest—Damien—jumped up and cheered. "Pizza, pizza, pizza."

"See what you did?" she murmured.

Rhydian grinned and then winked. "They can be spoiled tonight. It's a special occasion, after all."

At the amusement dancing in his eyes, she couldn't help but laugh. "Fine. But you'd better save me some. I'm starving, and if I'm feeding and getting Lorraine ready for bed, I won't be able to fend for myself like normal. I hope the next one is a girl, too. I need someone to balance out the numbers."

Rhydian merely winked again—probably to remind her dragon-shifters tended to have more male children than female—and rounded up the boys before guiding them to the kitchen.

As Delaney settled down in a chair with a view of the kitchen, she quickly had her daughter latched and eating. She watched her four lads as they argued over pizza toppings and she smiled. Who knew being tossed and locked inside a prison cell all those years ago would've given Delaney her happy ending.

Author's Note

I hope you enjoyed learning about the Welsh clan! We'll actually be back to Snowridge in Stonefire Dragons Universe #4, *Masked Dragon of Snowridge*. Rhydian and Delaney will also show up every now and again in my other books. :)

If you couldn't tell by first Clan Skyhunter, and now with Clan Snowridge, we've had stories set in all the UK clans except for Northcastle in Northern Ireland. I will write about them eventually, featuring Adrian Conroy and Elsie Day. However, I'm not sure if it'll be #5 or #6 in this series. (I have a doctor on Skyhunter I want to write about, too!)

But if you're interested to read about some American dragons, I do have a dragon spinoff novella series set near Lake Tahoe in the USA. The first book is called *The Dragon's Choice*.

As always, I have people to thank in helping me get this out:

• Becky Johnson and her team at Hot Tree Editing

always push me to do the best. Becky really had some valid concerns during edits, and Delaney and Rhydian's story is so much stronger because of it.

• My beta readers are amazing at capturing typos and minor inconsistencies. Huge thanks to Donna H., Iliana G., Sabrina D., and Sandy H.

And of course, a huge thank you to you, the reader, for either enjoying my dragons for the first time, or for following me from my longer books to this series. Writing is the best job in the world and it's your support that makes it so I can keep doing it.

Until next time, happy reading!
Cheers,
Jessie

Finding Dragon's Court

STONEFIRE DRAGONS UNIVERSE #3

To the world, Dr. Maximilian Holbrook projects himself as a chatty buffoon. It ensures everyone underestimates him, especially when it comes to his rivals. And it's worked, too, until an Australian dragon-shifter starts outsmarting him. That she's a woman doesn't matter to him. No, he'll do whatever it takes to find the legendary Dragon's Court, even if it means chaining her up to keep her out of the way.

Dr. Lavinia Walker overcame her past to become one of the best dragon-shifter archaeologists in Australia. So much so, she manages to snag a rare visa to excavate in the UK. It's been a life-long dream to discover the ruins of Queen Alviva's descendants and to finally shed light on what the dragons did once the Romans left Britain. She's so close to locating it but has one problem —a human male who's as determined as she is. When he plays dirty, she does too.

However, when a kiss changes their lives, Max and Lavinia have to decide if they are more to each other than mere rivals. As they race against the clock to solve the last clue, will they be able to work together? Or are they both too stubborn to give up and risk any chance of a future with each other?

Finding Dragon's Court is available in paperback.

About the Author

Jessie Donovan has sold over half a million books, has given away hundreds of thousands more to readers for free, and has even hit the *NY Times* and *USA Today* bestseller lists. She is best known for her dragon-shifter series, but also writes about elemental magic users, alien warriors, and even has a crazy romantic comedy series set in Scotland. When not reading a book, attempting to tame her yard, or traipsing around some foreign country on a shoestring, she can often be found interacting with her readers on Facebook. She lives near Seattle, where, yes, it rains a lot but it also makes everything green.

Visit her website at: www.JessieDonovan.com